THE ACRE SERIES

Almond and the Lanista
(A Miles and the Soldier Novella Book 2.1)

This edition published in 2023 by TB5 Publishing

gjkemp.co.uk

ISBN 978-1-915379-08-5 (paperback)
ISBN 978-1-915379-11-5 (ebook)

ACKNOWLEDGMENTS

To my incredible team who have helped get this novella out. Jess and Isabelle, for your guidance. My editors, Claire from Cherry Edits and Andy from The Narrative Craft. Andrei for your wonderful cover. Latifa (@latifahdesign) for all your design work. And Ashley for all your hard work on my socials.

Thank you.

THE ACRE SERIES

Thank you for your interest in The Acre Series. I recommend you read the principal novels in order as the characters and the story grow with the series. The novellas are prequels and sequels to the principal novels. You can read them in any order you wish.

—

The Acre Series

Principal Books

Juno and the Lady (An Acre Story Book 1)

Miles and the Soldier (An Acre Story Book 2)

Juno and the Lady Novellas

Valen and the Beasts: A Juno and the Lady Novella (An Acre Story Book 1.1)

Petra and the Sewer Rats: A Juno and the Lady Novella (An Acre Story Book 1.2)

Miles and the Soldier Novellas

Almond and the Lanista: A Miles and the Soldier Novella

(An Acre Story Book 2.1)

CHAPTER 1

THE LANISTA

'Come here, boy,' Almond said, slapping his knee. 'It's time to go home.'

The small brown-haired dog sprang out of the stream and shook himself, scattering droplets of water in every direction. With his tongue hanging out, he scampered up the riverbank, ran over to Almond, and licked his hand.

'Going to give you a bit of a clean when we get home, aren't we, boy?' Almond said, squeezing the dog's ear.

The small dog growled and stretched as he looked up at Almond with big brown eyes.

'Off we go then, Scrappy. Lead the way,' Almond said, pointing up the path.

Scrappy bolted off with his tail wagging furiously. Halfway up, he skidded to a halt, lay flat on his stomach, and sniffed the air.

'Leave the squirrels alone,' Almond said, following Scrappy up the path. 'You have terrorised them more than enough today.'

Scrappy growled more loudly. Almond jogged up to him and crouched. Scrappy sniffed the air again. The shrubs in the direction they faced rustled. A deep rumble sounded from behind them.

'Go, Scrappy,' Almond shouted, charging up the path. 'Run!'

A growling roar and padded paws came from somewhere beyond.

'Faster,' Almond shouted. 'Move, you silly dog.'

Branches and bushes snapped and popped behind them. Almond sucked in deep breaths of air as he sprinted up the path. Scrappy overtook Almond with his little legs pumping and his tiny tail stuck between his legs. The beast's roar sounded a little further away as Almond and Scrappy created more distance. Almond looked over his shoulder, then slowed. The thick black fur of the massive beast disappeared into the shrubs.

Scrappy skidded to a halt, turned, and let loose a stream of high-pitched barks.

'Oh, now you are all tough, aren't you, little one?' Almond said, a smile spreading across his face. 'Come on. Let's go home before it gets dark. That beast will continue stalking us and he will have us both for dinner.'

Scrappy trotted next to Almond as they walked down the narrow path. About an hour later, they turned west onto a wide cobblestone road. Small weeds poked their heads through the gaps in the unkempt cobbles.

Almond rubbed the tiny medallion on the chain hanging from his neck. 'Not many people come this far south anymore, do they, Scrappy? It used to be full of tradesmen.'

Scrappy jumped up and tried to lick Almond's hand.

'A couple more hours and we will be home. We have enough fish for a week,' Almond said, holding up the net. 'As soon as we get home, I will salt them, so they last for a good few days.'

Scrappy's tongue lolled out as he looked up at the fish. A flash of light streaked across the sky. A long, distant rumble of thunder rolled across the southern lands.

'You can tell how far away the storm is. Count from the moment you see the lightning to when you hear the thunder,'

Almond said, bending over and patting Scrappy on the side. 'But don't forget to divide the number by five.'

Scrappy jumped and snapped at the fish.

'Ha,' Almond said, lifting the fish above his head. 'Got to be quicker than that.'

Another fork of lightning flashed through the sky.

'One thousand, two thousand, three thousand, four thousand, five—'

The rumble of thunder filled their ears.

'Closer than I thought,' Almond said, looking up at the sky, his face etched with worry. 'We need to pick up the pace. Lightning kills many people each year.'

Scrappy barked at the sky.

'And a few doggies,' Almond said, smiling down at Scrappy. 'Come on, little one, let's pick up the pace.'

As they hurried along the darkening road, Almond nervously scanned the bushes on either side, checking for movement. Another white fork of lightning flashed across the sky. Almost immediately, the thunder slammed into their ears. Scrappy yelped and ran in between Almond's legs. The winds began to gust, blowing loose leaves across the road.

'When the winds stop, the rain will come,' Almond said, breaking into a run. 'Come on Scraps, we are almost home.'

Scrappy narrowed his eyes as the gusting wind pinned his small ears against the back of his head. Another white fork of lightning cut through the sky. Scrappy whimpered and darted off in front of Almond.

'Here we are,' Almond said, rounding a bend and kicking open their small gate. 'Let's get into the house quickly.'

Scrappy darted through the gate and up the three steps to the cottage's small wooden door. Thunder cracked overhead. Almond ran up the steps and ripped open the door. He watched Scrappy dart into the house and disappear into the darkness of the small room at the back.

Almond pulled the door closed behind him. 'Time to get a fire going, Scraps. It will be a lot better with some light and warmth.'

A muffled thud sounded from the back room.

'Scraps?' Almond said, frowning. 'What are you up to?'

The small dog yelped.

'Who is there?' Almond said, reaching for the knife in his belt.

'I wouldn't do that if I were you,' a man said.

Almond spread his feet and willed his eyes to adjust to the light. 'What do you want?'

Scrappy let out another yelp.

'If you hurt my dog, I will hurt you,' Almond said, his voice lowering.

'Your dog is as good as dead,' the man said. 'You are coming with us.'

Almond pulled out his knife and stalked towards the dark room. The floorboards creaked behind him. He spun around and slashed his knife at a massive bearded man.

Scrappy yelped behind him.

'Leave my dog alone,' Almond yelled, turning and facing the dark room.

A loud crack sounded through the small cottage. Almond's knees buckled as white dots filled his vision.

'Load him into the cart,' he heard one of them say.

Slowly, the darkness took him. Scrappy's yelps filled his ears.

A big raindrop slammed against the side of Almond's temple. He opened his eyes slowly and groaned as he ran his hand along the back of his head. Dried blood crumbled under his fingertips.

'Where am I?' Almond croaked as his eyes came into focus.

A man with no teeth, matted hair, and blackened fingernails stared down at him. Metal bars surrounded him and a dirty blanket lay underneath him. The sound of a horse's nicker broke the rhythmic pattern of hooves on the cobblestone road.

'Where am I?' he said, more loudly.

The man with no teeth lifted a finger and placed it on his lips. Almond dug his elbow into the blanket and pushed himself up. The cart hit a raised cobble, causing it to rattle and bounce.

'Where are you taking me?' Almond shouted, placing his hand on his head. 'Let me out of here right now!'

'He is awake, boss,' the bearded man said.

Almond turned his head and curled a lip at the massive man atop an enormous horse.

'Hey you, bearded man,' Almond said, jabbing his chin at the man on the horse. 'Let me go.'

The man chuckled. 'He wants to be let go, boss.'

'Tell him to shut his talking or we will put him back to sleep,' a man said from the front of the cart.

Almond shook his head again, this time finally clearing the haze from his mind. All around him, rolling hills stretched as far as he could see. The thunderstorm, now leaving them behind, had become a fine mist. The cart's wheels groaned and moaned as it tried to cut through the thick mud on the cobblestone path.

'Where is Scrappy?' Almond said.

The bearded man looked away.

'What have you done with my dog?'

Still, the bearded man did not turn his head.

Almond stared at him. 'Tell me where my dog is.'

The man who sat on the cart's front bench turned and said, 'Don't worry. It was quick. The dog is in a much better place.'

'I will make you both pay,' Almond growled. 'My dog did nothing to you.'

The bearded man pulled his horse closer to the cart. With one movement, he pulled a pole from his saddle and jabbed it hard into Almond's ribs. Almond's elbow gave way, and with a thump, he collapsed onto the blanket.

'Say something else and I will put you to sleep,' the bearded man said.

'Leave him be,' the man in the front said. 'Let him cry for his stupid dog.'

The bearded man looked away. 'Yes, boss.'

Almond curled into a ball. His body shook as anger coursed through his veins. The sleeve of his shirt wafted a faint smell of Scrappy into his nostrils. Almond grabbed the medallion around his neck and brought it up to his mouth. The man with no teeth placed a hand on Almond's shoulder and squeezed. He looked down at Almond with kind, knowing eyes. Almond gave the man a small smile, then curled up in a ball, falling in and out of consciousness for the next few hours. Eventually, a sunbeam pierced through the clouds and gently touched Almond's eyelids. He shook his head, then pushed himself up onto his elbow. He placed the back of his hand over his eyes to block the sun's bright rays.

'Not long now, boss,' the bearded man said. 'I remember these hills.'

The man in the front jabbed his thumb at the people in the cage. 'We will not get much for this lot. They are a sorry bunch.'

'I don't think you will get much for the small man,' the bearded one said, looking at Almond. 'Someone has broken him. I can see it in his eyes.'

'Look at the size of his hands,' the man in the front said. 'I think he will make a good server at the lanista's table.'

The bearded man shook his head at Almond. 'I think he is still crying for his dog, boss.'

'Leave him be,' the man in the front said. 'We should get to Ludus Capri before dark.'

The bearded man rattled his lips. 'Off to Battleacre after, boss? We have been on the road for months.'

'That depends on how many of these we sell,' the man in the front said, jabbing his finger at them again. 'If we have men left, we go to the next ludus.'

The bearded man's face dropped. 'You know we will not sell all of them.'

The man in the front waved dismissively.

Almond sat up and glared at the bearded man. He grabbed the medallion around his neck and rubbed it.

The bearded man raised an eyebrow. 'What have you got there, little man? It looks all nice and shiny.'

'You killed my dog,' Almond said, his voice lowering. 'The only reason you are not dead is because of this medallion.'

'Shut up, you two,' the man in the front said. 'We are close to Ludus Capri and the last thing I need the lanista to hear is you two grumbling like children.'

'I will make you both pay for what you did,' Almond said, his voice raising.

The crunch of the pole against the back of Almond's head echoed through the rolling hills. Almond collapsed onto the blanket and groaned.

The toothless man leant in and whispered into Almond's ear. 'Keep quiet, man. If you carry on like this, you might get one of us killed.'

Almond raised a hand. 'Sorry, I am just angry.'

The man nodded. 'I understand.'

Almond lay on the blanket and looked up at the bars criss-crossing the cart's roof.

'What is that medallion?' the man with no teeth said.

Almond turned his head. 'It's a promise.'

The toothless man nodded and sat back.

'There it is,' the bearded man said. 'Ludus Capri.'

Everyone in the cart turned and looked up the hill. On the top of a small ridge, several fortified houses looked down at them. From inside the walls, the clash of steel and the shouts of men filtered out and down the valley.

'Ride up ahead and tell them we are here,' the man at the front said to the bearded one.

The bearded man jabbed his heels into the side of his horse and rode up the hill. Almond sat up and watched him wind up the slope to the large gate.

'What is this place?' a young boy whispered from the back of the cart.

'Gladiators,' a man said. 'It's where they train gladiators. The school is called a ludus.'

'It is owned by someone called a lanista,' another man said. 'He trains the gladiators for the games.'

'They are going to use us to practise on,' another man said. 'We will be dead in a day.'

Almond looked back up the hill. The bearded man sat on his horse, waiting. Eventually, the gate screeched open. The bearded man spoke to someone, then waved and smiled down at the cart.

'I don't want to die,' the young boy said.

'Steady lad,' another man said. 'We are not dying today.'

The young boy pulled his knees up to his chest. He laid the side of his head against his knees so nobody could see the tears running down his face. Almond looked away and sighed.

The man at the front of the cart stood and waved. 'Hello there, sir.'

'Good evening, sir,' a tall thin man shouted from the wall. 'I see you bring His Lordship some more spoils.'

'Indeed we do, brother,' the man at the front said. 'Getting harder to find quality these days, though.'

The tall thin man nodded. 'They look like a band of starving idiots. Not sure the boss is going to want to do anything with this lot.'

'I will take anything right now,' the man at the front said.

The cart lurched forward and continued its way up the hill. The horses turned into the main entrance of the ludus and pulled the cart into the courtyard.

'Good evening, my lord,' the man at the front said.

'Good evening,' a man with a deep voice answered. 'It has been a while since I have seen you.'

'Yes, lanista,' the man said. 'To find these people, we go far and wide, which takes time, sir.'

'If it's not the vampires, it's the wolves,' the lanista said. 'Many people are travelling to a place in the south. Fairacre, I think they call it.'

'Never been there myself,' the man in the front said.

'Show me what you have,' the lanista said.

'I am afraid I don't have much for you,' the man said, turning and signalling to the bearded one.

The bearded man signalled to two heavy-set guards, who went around the back of the cart and swung the metal door open.

'Out, out,' the guards shouted, pulling the people out of the cart. 'Stand over there.'

Almond dragged himself to the edge of the cart, jumped to the ground, and walked to the line of people. He turned and peered at the bearded man through his eyebrows.

'What are you looking at, slave?' the bearded man said with a sneer.

'I am going to make you pay,' Almond said.

The crack of wood against flesh echoed through the valley. Almond fell to his knees with a gasp. The guard standing behind him took a step back.

'Let's get on with this,' the man from the front of the cart said.

Almond felt two pairs of hands rough him to his feet.

The lanista walked up the line and looked the first man over. Apparently not seeing anything he liked, he moved to the next man. He reviewed him, then moved to the next.

The man from the front of the cart cleared his throat. 'Not even this man, sir? He is strong.'

The lanista ignored him and moved to the next man, then the next, where he stopped. He inclined his head. Two guards walked up, grabbed the man, and dragged him to the side. The lanista continued his inspection. Almond seized the opportunity and darted away from the line. He charged at the bearded man. A foot away from slamming his fist into the man's face, he crashed to the ground as two guards tackled him.

'Look at me,' Almond shouted. 'Remember this face. One day I will find you and I will make you pay.'

The bearded man threw back his head and howled with laughter.

'What is going on here?' the lanista said, walking out from his guards' protection.

'It is nothing, sir,' the cart owner said. 'This weasel of a man is upset because one of my men killed his dog.'

'Why did you kill his dog?' the lanista said, walking over to where Almond struggled against the guards.

'Bloody thing wouldn't stop attacking us,' the bearded man said. 'Plus, we knew we were going to take him. Why leave the poor doggie on his own?'

Almond snarled and spat.

'It is wise never to come between a man and his dog,' the lanista said. 'I like the fight in this one. Take him to the other line.'

'Are you sure, sir?' the cart owner said, his eyes wide.

The lanista spun on his heel and walked back to the line. He continued his inspection of the men. Almond tore his eyes away from the bearded man and watched the graceful lanista go through his selection.

'Look at me, boy,' the lanista said to the young boy who didn't want to die.

The young boy hung his head.

'Look at him,' a guard said, smacking the boy on the back of the head.

The young boy looked up.

The lanista seemed to think for a second, then moved to the next man.

'He is a good boy,' Almond shouted. 'He will serve you well.'

'Shut up,' a guard said, driving the hilt of his sword into Almond's stomach.

The lanista spun around and walked over to Almond. He bent over until his face was inches from Almond's. 'You are either very brave or very stupid. Why keep talking when you know they will beat you?'

Almond narrowed his eyes at the lanista but said nothing.

'Hmm,' the lanista said, straightening his back and rubbing his chin. 'Send the boy over to the line.'

'Leave me alone,' the boy said as he struggled to free himself from the guards. 'I don't want to die.'

The lanista chuckled. 'I can see why you like the boy. He has your spirit.'

'Don't hurt him,' Almond said. 'He is just a boy.'

The guard yelped. 'He just stamped on my toe.'

The lanista shook his head at the guard. 'He is just a boy. Control him.'

'Stop struggling,' Almond said to the boy.

The boy stopped. The guard marched him over to stand next to Almond.

Almond waited for the guard to stand back. 'What is your name?'

The boy kept his mouth shut.

The lanista got to the end of the line, turned, and walked back to where the cart owner stood. 'This is a sorry bunch of people. Take the rest of them to the other lanistae.'

'I am sorry, sir,' the cart owner said. 'There are not that many strong people left. They have escaped to Battleacre or the City of Lynn.'

The lanista signalled to the tall thin man who walked over and handed him a small white pouch.

'There is extra in there for you, as I know times are hard,' the lanista said, handing the pouch to the cart owner.

The man weighed the small bag in his hand. 'That is very generous of you, sir. I appreciate it.'

The lanista signalled to four armed guards who ran up to the line of six men.

'You cannot let him go,' Almond shouted.

The lanista arched an eyebrow. 'Let who go?'

'That man,' Almond said, pointing to the bearded man. 'He killed my Scrappy.'

'Oh, shut your moaning,' the bearded man said, climbing onto his horse. 'The dog was old and near death, anyway.'

'He was not old,' Almond shouted. 'He was my best friend.'

He clucked his tongue and jabbed his heels into the side of his horse. He sighed at Almond. 'I am sorry about your silly dog.'

Almond felt like someone had punched him in the stomach. He looked up at the bearded man with tears in his eyes.

'Let's go,' the cart owner said. 'We need to get to the next lanista by sunrise.'

The four guards guided Almond, the four men, and the young boy through an archway and into an enormous hall. Four well-dressed guards stood to attention in each of the hall's corners. They bowed their heads as the lanista walked in.

'Get these six washed and ready for placement,' the lanista said to a tall thin man. 'I will be back in an hour.'

'They will be ready for you in the square, sir,' the thin man said with a gravelly voice.

'Thank you, Erik,' the lanista said.

The four guards who had led them into the hall marched back out through the door.

'Follow me,' Erik said.

Almond hesitated and eyed the hall's exit.

'You can run if you wish, but they will cut you down before you reach the estate walls,' Erik said, pointing a finger at one guard. 'The lanista has them stationed inside the halls and on top of the estate wall. He also has bowmen who are extremely accurate.'

As they exited the hall, Almond ran his eyes along the estate walls and spotted the bowmen hiding in the shadows. Almond gave up on escape and followed Erik and the others over a wide courtyard and through a steel door. They walked down a winding stone staircase and into a wide hall. Closed doors on each wall gave the impression of a big prison.

'What is this place?' Almond said.

'Gladiators quarters,' Erik said.

'I told you we were fodder,' a man said. 'We will not see the morning, I promise you that.'

'I don't want to die,' the young boy said.

Erik looked over his shoulder. 'None of you are going to die tonight. Stop the dramatics.'

The man sneered at Erik. 'You would say that.'

At the end of the hall, they descended another winding stone staircase. Erik tilted his head to one side to avoid the sloping roof. At the bottom of the staircase, they continued along a narrower corridor until they walked into another large hall. Unlike the one above, this hall was filled with activity. Pots and pans banged, saws and blades cut, and water sloshed. Men and women called to each other as they went about their business.

'The kitchen,' Erik said. 'Follow me. The baths are at the back.'

At the back of the massive hall, they walked through another narrow corridor and out into a small hall filled with hot, steaming pools.

'These are the baths shared by everyone,' Erik said. 'You shall respect them as we all use them.'

The six undressed. One by one, they walked into the large steaming baths. Almond felt his whole body relax as the scented, steaming water soaked his limbs.

'There is soap in the holders along the sides,' Erik said. 'Clean yourselves well. There are clothes at the back when you have finished.'

Almond dunked his head under the water and washed his hair with the bar of soap. Caked mud flaked off, leaving the water a light brown. A few minutes later, he made his way to the back of the bathing hall, where he walked up the steps and to the long concrete shelf lining the wall. After drying himself off with a towel, he found a white cotton robe and some tie-up sandals. The young boy climbed out of the bath and covered himself quickly with a towel. He searched the concrete shelf until he found some cotton trousers and a long-sleeved cotton shirt.

'Are you feeling better?' Almond said. 'You still haven't told me your name.'

The boy glanced over at Erik.

'He cannot hear you from here,' Almond said.

'My name is Jarod,' the boy said. 'Please don't tell anyone.'

Almond frowned. 'Why don't you want anyone to know?'

'You two, hurry,' Erik called. 'We meet the lanista in ten minutes.'

'What is your name?' Jarod said.

'Almond.' He walked along the side of the bath. 'Pleased to meet you, kid.'

Erik lined up the five men and one boy and cast a critical eye over each. He lifted his nose and smelt the air. With a nod, he turned on his heel and made for the narrow corridor. They back-tracked the way they had come until they walked through the arch into the main courtyard. A man walked along the sides of the square, lighting oil lamps. The light flickered, sending long shadows up the wall.

'Stand in a line and keep quiet, please,' Erik said.

The six stood in a line and waited.

Exactly on time, the lanista appeared and walked up to the line of men. 'Well done, Erik. They look and smell a lot better.'

Erik gave a small bow.

'Welcome to my house,' the lanista said. 'I have paid the slave catcher for you, therefore you belong to me.'

'I am no slave,' one man said.

The lanista turned and waved a hand at the estate gate. 'You are free to leave if you wish.'

With a glimmer of fear, the man hung his head.

'We will give you jobs to do,' the lanista said. 'In return, I will feed you, clothe you and protect you. All I wish is for your loyalty to my house. Do you understand?'

Almond lifted a defiant chin. Jarod, seeing Almond lift his chin, did the same. The lanista looked at them with a bemused expression. A few moments later, the lanista walked up to the first man in the line. 'Strong and young,' he said, looking him over. 'I will test you in the gladiator circle.'

'Follow that guard,' Erik said, pointing the man in the guard's direction.

'Servants quarters,' the lanista said to the next man.

Erik pointed his finger.

'Gladiator circle for the next two,' the lanista said.

Erik again pointed his finger.

The lanista walked up to Jarod.

Jarod looked up at the lanista with narrowed eyes and an attempt at a brave face.

'It seems this youngster has found some bravery, Erik,' the lanista said.

'Leave him alone,' Almond said.

'I would advise you to treat me with some respect, slave,' the lanista said, shaking his head. 'I could have let this boy be gladiator fodder.'

Almond looked at Jarod, then hung his head.

'You will serve my lady's household,' the lanista said to Jarod.

Jarod stared, unmoving.

'And as for you, I think it's to the gladiator circle for you,' the lanista said, looking at Almond.

Erik thumbed over his shoulder for Jarod to go in the direction he pointed.

'You will be fine,' Almond said, seeing Jarod panic. 'Just do as you are told.'

Jarod nodded and followed the guard into the hall.

'Follow that guard,' Erik said, indicating a guard to Almond.

Almond watched Jarod disappear down a corridor, then made his way over to his assigned guard. The guard turned and escorted him and three others through a long passage. A few moments later, they exited the passage and stood in a large sandy ring.

'This is my training arena,' the lanista said, appearing out of the passageway. 'Here, my taskmasters will train you in the art of fighting. If you do not rise to the challenge, they will remove your head.'

The three men and Almond scanned the arena.

'See them off to get food and then to their quarters, Erik,' the lanista said. 'We will start early tomorrow morning.'

'What of Jarod?' Almond said. 'I should not have spoken out of turn and I hope the young boy will not suffer because of it.'

'We will look after the young boy,' the lanista said. 'When he grows, though, they will test him to see if he can be a gladiator.'

Almond inclined his head. 'I thank you, sir.'

'Finally,' the lanista said, throwing up his hands. 'At least one of them is calling me sir, right, Erik?'

'Yes, sir,' Erik said, a thin smile playing across his lips.

'Get them fed and off to bed,' the lanista said, disappearing down the corridor.

'Follow me back to the baths,' Erik said. 'Your quarters are to the left of them.'

Almond and the others followed Erik down into the depths of the estate. At the second floor below ground level, he turned left just before the baths and walked down another passage. At the end of the passage, they broke out into a wide room with doors lining the walls. In the centre of the wide room sat four long tables with chairs on either side.

'Sit,' Erik said, waving at the chairs.

As the last of the four sat, several servants walked into the room carrying plates and pitchers. Almond stared at the mound of food in front of him.

'Eat,' Erik said, frustration rising in his voice.

'This may be our last meal,' one man said, digging into his food.

Almond watched as the three men devoured the food in front of them. He pushed his plate away and with his head in his hands, he rested his elbows on the table.

'You pine for your animal?' Erik said, towering above him. 'I am sorry for your loss. I, too, miss my dog.'

Almond let out a sigh. 'I want to take the head of the man who killed my dog. He does not deserve to live. But I swore an oath to never kill another man again.'

'Eat and keep your strength up, for you may one day cross paths with him again,' Erik said.

Almond reluctantly reached for the plate of food. Picking up a fork, he ate as much as his stomach would allow. The rest of the food he passed to the three men.

'I have made arrangements for you to share a room with the boy,' Erik said, looking at Almond. 'It is in our interests to put him with someone where he will be safe.'

Almond pushed the chair from underneath him and stood. 'That is kind of you, Erik.'

Erik pointed to a door in the hall's corner.

Almond walked briskly to the door and swung it open. On a small cot in the corner, Jarod slept soundly. Almond looked up at the bedroom walls that stood three men high. On the farthest wall, a long, thin window let in a stream of moonlight. Almond walked up to the second bed, kicked his sandals off, and lay on his back. He interlaced his fingers behind his head and stared at the ceiling. After a few minutes, his eyes closed.

CHAPTER 2
SCRAPPY

Almond jerked awake and sat up.

'What?' Jarod said, jumping with fright.

'Did you hear that?' Almond said.

Jarod sat up on his cot and frowned at Almond. 'I don't think I heard anything. What did you hear?'

A noise came from the window at the top of the room. They both looked up at the same time.

'I heard it,' Jarod said. 'Sounds like something is trying to get through the window.'

A whine sounded, followed by more scratching.

'Is that a dog?' Jarod said.

Almond got to his feet and squinted up at the window. Small pieces of dirt trickled down through the air. The scratching got louder. Another whine.

'That definitely sounds like a dog,' Jarod said.

Someone banged on their door. 'Time to get moving and time for breakfast,' Erik called through to them.

Almond grabbed his sandals and pulled them on. He hurried to the door and swung it open.

Erik took a step back in surprise, then marched forward with his weapon raised.

'Whoa, steady,' Jarod said, jumping in front of Almond.

'I heard a dog whine from the window,' Almond said. 'I need to check if it is Scrappy.'

Erik frowned. 'Your dog is dead. And if he was alive, how would he be here?'

'It sounded like Scrappy,' Almond said. 'I can tell from the whine.'

'There are a lot of dogs around here,' Erik said. 'Get your breakfast, then make your way to the gladiator circle.'

Almond grabbed Erik's sleeve. He raised his weapon again.

Jarod frantically waved his arms. 'Can you stop doing that?'

'It will only take me a few minutes,' Almond said. 'Please, can I check? He might be injured.'

'That window leads to the outside,' Erik said. 'Everybody has to stay inside. It is the lanista's orders. Get your breakfast or I will lock you in your room for the day.'

'Can you at least ask the lanista?' Almond said.

Erik's eyes disappeared under his brow. 'Get your breakfast, slave. This is your last warning.'

'Come on,' Jarod said, grabbing Almond by the hand. 'Let's get some breakfast and see what we can do later.'

Almond stared at Erik in disbelief as Jarod dragged him to the long tables. He flopped onto one of the chairs and watched the servants bring bowls of oats and thick honey.

'Do you think it was your dog?' Jarod said from across the table.

Almond rubbed his face with both hands, then sighed deeply. 'I don't know. Maybe I just want it to be my dog.'

Jarod swallowed a spoonful of porridge. 'I will ask the ladies of the house if we can check. I am sure they will help if I ask nicely.'

'Don't get yourself into trouble,' Almond said. 'Remember, we are slaves in this place.'

'I will be careful,' Jarod said. 'As long as you promise to be careful in the gladiator circle.'

Almond nodded. 'I won't be fighting, so there isn't anything to worry about.'

Almond finished his food, said goodbye to Jarod, then followed a guard out of the building and into the courtyard. With not a cloud in sight, the sun's rays hurt his eyes. Almond followed the long passageway until he reached the arena. Gladiators and servants of all shapes and sizes practised in the circle. Puffs of sand blasted into the air as defeated gladiators and servants fell into the dirt.

'Over here, servant,' Erik said, waving Almond over.

Almond walked over to Erik and sat on one of the concrete steps skirting the arena. 'Why are the servants fighting with each other?'

Erik looked at Almond with surprise. 'Don't you know how the games work?'

'I have heard of them but never watched or partaken in them,' Almond said.

A gladiator hit the ground in front of them. Blood trickled from the corner of his mouth. A monstrous man stood above him, wielding a massive wooden practice sword.

'Be careful, Hans,' Erik said. 'The lanista will not take kindly to you destroying his property.'

Hans looked at Erik and grunted. He spun on his heel and looked for the next gladiator to fight.

'There are two types of battles in the arenas,' Erik said. 'Gladiator versus gladiator and gladiator and servant versus gladiator and servant.'

'Servants fight inside the arena?' Almond said, his mouth falling open.

'Yes,' Erik said. 'The gladiator and servant work as a team.'

Almond's eyes widened. 'You don't think the lanista has me earmarked to be a fighting servant?'

'I certainly do,' the lanista said, walking up behind them.

Erik rose and bowed. 'Good morning, sir,' he said. 'I hope you are well.'

The lanista gave Erik a nod. 'I am well, thank you, Erik. It is time to see what our new recruits can do.'

'Yes, sir,' Erik said, walking into the centre of the arena. 'Halt,' he said. 'Our lanista will be entering the ring.'

Every gladiator and servant stopped fighting and watched the lanista join Erik.

'Join us,' Erik said, pointing to Almond and the other three recruits. 'Come on, hurry up and stand in a straight line.'

Almond and the other three recruits walked into the middle of the arena and stood in a line in front of the lanista.

The lanista looked the four men over. 'We will hand you a sword and shield. If you prove worthy, we will train you as a gladiator of Ludus Capri.'

Servants ran to the weapons rack and returned holding swords and shields. The three other men grabbed a set of weapons each. Almond stood staring at the weapons in the servants' hands.

'Make your choice, servant,' the lanista said to him. 'You can fight with nothing if you wish.'

'I don't know how to fight,' Almond said, looking up at the lanista. 'I am a farmer.'

'Pick up a weapon,' a gladiator said, shoving Almond in the back. 'Better to have one than none at all.'

Almond let out a long sigh before grabbing a sword and shield from one of the servants.

The lanista signalled to the magistrus to begin the testing.

'All to the side of the arena,' the magistrus bellowed. 'Move now.'

Almond backtracked until his back hit the high wall of the arena.

'You,' the magistrus said, pointing to one of the new men. 'You will fight Ned.'

A middle-sized gladiator wielding a small trainer axe and shield walked into the middle of the arena. He looked up into the sky, growled loudly, then slammed his axe against his shield. The new man walked into the ring's centre, where he pointed his sword at Ned. With a howl, Ned launched himself into the air and swung his practice axe. The man dodged and jabbed his sword, stabbing Ned in the shoulder. Ned backed off and narrowed his eyes.

'I may not be as big as you, but I can fight,' the man said.

Over the next ten minutes, the two men traded blow for blow. Blood dripped down their cheeks and noses as the impact wounds opened their skin.

'Halt,' the magistrus shouted.

'Well,' the lanista said, looking at the magistrus, 'are you satisfied with his skill?'

The magistrus slammed his fist against his chest and gave the lanista a nod.

Erik clapped his hands. 'Good news, then. You shall join the ranks as a novicius. Ned will be your mentor.'

Ned walked up to the man and held out a hand. The men gripped forearms and shook.

'Next,' the lanista said.

The second man fell to his knees after one side blow from the gladiator's club. He whimpered and slumped to the ground where he lay on his side.

The magistrus looked at the lanista and shook his head.

'Servants quarters,' the lanista muttered. 'What a waste of money. Cannot even be a servant fighter.'

The man pulled himself to his feet and exited the arena circle.

'Next,' the lanista shouted.

'Your turn,' Erik said, pointing at Almond.

Almond took in a deep breath, pushed himself off the wall, and went to stand in the middle of the arena. A moment later, he lay face-down in the sand. Blood poured out of a gash on the top of his head. A gladiator servant stood over him with a blood-soaked sword.

'He is holding back,' the magistrus said. 'Get him up and we go again!'

The guards pulled Almond roughly to his feet. The gladiator servant charged Almond, who dodged to one side, narrowly missing the swinging sword. Almond slashed at the servant, but hit nothing. The servant spun, bounced to his other foot, and slammed the edge of his sword into Almond's side. With a gush of air from his lungs, Almond collapsed onto the ground.

'Get him up,' the magistrus said. 'We go again. You are holding back. We know you can fight.'

The guards pulled Almond to his feet.

'Almond,' Jarod shouted. 'What does your dog look like?'

Everyone in the arena spun and stared at the boy.

'You should be serving the lanista's family, boy,' Erik shouted, rising to his full height. 'Get out of here and do your job.'

'What does your dog look like, Almond?' Jarod shouted again.

'Small, with short brown hair and a white spot on his head. He also has black socks,' Almond said, wincing and sucking in some air.

'He is alive!' Jarod shouted. 'He is outside the walls.'

'Get him out of here!' Erik shouted, pointing at Jarod.

Almond turned to the lanista. 'I would like to see if my dog is alive.'

'Only if he fights,' the magistrus interrupted. 'He goes nowhere until he shows us what he can do.'

'Please, I would like to see if my dog is alive,' Almond said.

The lanista shook his head. 'The magistrus runs the arena. He will not release you until you show him what you can do. We all know you can fight. You have a warrior's stance.'

'I made a promise,' Almond said, rubbing his fingers over his medallion. 'I promised someone I would never hurt anyone again.'

'Your choice, slave,' the magistrus said. 'You fight and you can see if it is your dog, or you don't fight and you stay a servant until you die.'

Almond hung his head for a second, then looked up into the sky. 'Please forgive me, my love.'

'Fight, slave!' the magistrus shouted, stepping back.

'If I am going to fight, I am going to make someone pay for it,' Almond said, picking up his sword and shield and pointing it at the magistrus. 'Let's see what type of spine you have, old man.'

The magistrus snorted. 'I wish not to hurt someone so small. Fight a servant, slave.'

Almond stalked towards the magistrus.

'Enough,' the lanista said. 'I will not have you fight my prized trainer.'

'Then who?' Almond said, spinning around.

The servant Almond was supposed to fight rushed forward. 'You dishonour me by not fighting me!' he shouted.

Almond sidestepped and flicked his sword. The servant collapsed face-first into the dirt. The arena fell silent.

'I knew he was holding back,' the magistrus said. 'You have a warrior's eye, a warrior's stance and a warrior's intelligence.'

Almond dropped the sword and shield. 'I would like to see if my dog is alive.'

The magistrus nodded at the lanista.

'Erik, make sure you cuff him and four guards escort him around the estate,' the lanista said. 'If it is indeed his dog, then capture it and bring it in.'

Erik gave the lanista a bow, then signalled to the guards. Four of them trotted over and surrounded Almond.

'Hands,' Erik said.

Almond held them out. He winced as the heavy cuffs clamped around his wrists.

Erik checked the cuffs then led the way through the passageway until they reached the courtyard where he signalled for the guards to open the gate.

'Where did they see him?' Erik said, looking at Jarod.

'They said he was west near our cell window,' Jarod said.

'Call him,' Erik said, moving north up the path. 'See if he recognises your voice.'

'Scrappy,' Almond yelled. 'Come here, boy.'

Erik signalled to the guards. 'Take us west to the cell window.'

They continued up the path, shouting Scrappy's name. Erik turned off the path and into the knee-high bushes. He used his cane to swish away any insects that buzzed up into the air.

'Scrappy,' Almond shouted, following Erik into the thickets.

A dog's whine sounded from somewhere in the bushes a few feet ahead of them.

'Keep quiet,' Almond shouted. 'I can hear something.'

Erik held up his hand. The guards stopped thrashing through the undergrowth and remained still.

A few seconds later, a whine sounded again.

Almond swished the bushes aside with his cuffed hands. A few steps forward, he dropped to a knee. 'Scrappy.'

The bright eyes of Scrappy looked up at him. Blood soaked his hind legs.

'He doesn't look too good,' Erik said, leaning over Almond's shoulders. 'There is a lot of blood.'

Almond turned his head and growled. 'Get away from him.'

Erik held a hand up and backed away.

Almond ran his hands along Scrappy until he found the wound. A thin gash spanned one of his hind legs. He carefully scooped the dog up and cradled him in his arms.

'Let's get back to the estate,' Erik said. 'Maybe the medicus can help.'

Almond hurried back through the bushes, down the path, and back into the estate's courtyard.

'Call the medicus,' Erik yelled at a guard.

The guard saluted, then disappeared down a passageway.

'Oh my,' a young lady said.

Almond turned around and stopped dead in his tracks. A beautiful young lady with long blonde hair stood in front of him.

'Is the little one OK?' she said, walking up to Almond. 'There is blood everywhere.'

'He has a long thin wound on his back leg,' Almond said.

'We will get the medicus to take a look,' the lady said. 'My name is Mahina, I am the lanista's daughter.'

Almond gave Mahina a quick bow. 'Will the medicus know what to do?'

'The medicus will know what to do,' Mahina said, smiling.

Another tall man walked into the courtyard. In his hand, he carried a large case that rattled as he walked.

'Medicus Pascal,' Mahina said, smiling sweetly at him. 'I trust you can help this small animal.'

'For once it is not you bringing me these beasts, Mahina,' Medicus Pascal said. 'Bring the dog to my rooms, please.'

Almond followed the medicus through the corridor and into the gladiator hall. Instead of continuing to the kitchen, he turned down a smaller corridor lined with doors. Halfway along, he opened a door into a room housing two enormous beds and a large metal table.

'Get that blanket, Mahina,' Medicus Pascal said. 'And place it on the table.'

Mahina grabbed the blanket and threw it across the table.

'Place the dog on the blanket,' Pascal said. 'Careful now.'

Almond placed Scrappy carefully on the table.

Pascal tutted at the wound on the dog. 'Some beast has chased him. He is lucky to be alive.'

'Are you saying a beast did this and not a man?' Almond said.

Pascal shook his head. 'This is a claw mark. Maybe a wolf or, even worse, a brown bear. See how thin it is?'

'Almond, you found him,' Jarod said, running into the room.

'Do not run into my rooms, boy,' Pascal growled.

'Sorry,' Jarod said, skidding to a halt. 'Is he your dog, Almond?'

'He is,' Almond said. 'He's my Scrappy.'

'Will he be OK?' Jarod said.

'He will be fine,' Pascal said. 'He has lost a lot of blood. The wound will heal pretty quickly.'

A knock on the door sounded.

'Yes,' Pascal said. 'What is it?'

A guard opened the door. 'The lanista is looking for the servant.'

'I am staying here with Scrappy,' Almond said.

'That is not a wise choice,' Mahina said. 'I will wait here with your dog. If we have anything to report, Jarod will come and find you.'

Almond looked at the fierce guard, then walked over to Scrappy and kissed the small dog on the top of the head. 'Sleep well, my friend.'

'The lanista is waiting for you, slave,' the guard said.

'Go,' Mahina said. 'My father does not like waiting for anybody.'

Almond followed the guard through the corridors, out into the courtyard, and down the long passageway to the arena.

'Your dog is still alive?' Erik said.

'He is,' Almond said, a small smile playing on his face. 'It looks like the bearded man did not kill him.'

The lanista appeared from the corridor, reading a scroll as he walked.

'What is it, sir?' Erik said.

The lanista waved the scroll. 'The General of Battleacre is holding games, and they have invited Ludus Capri.'

Erik held his breath.

'Yes, I know Erik. We will have to take the chance though, my friend,' the lanista said, rolling up the scroll.

Almond gave the lanista a confused look.

'Do you think we should take the chance?' the lanista said.

'Hans is looking good, sir,' Erik said. 'He is our champion and I have faith in him. Shall we ask for the magistrus's opinion?'

'The magistrus will always say we should go,' the lanista said, turning and looking into the arena. 'He is a fighter, a warrior, and the games will always call him.'

'Hans has always wanted to fight for a place in the Queen's Guard,' Erik said. 'I think we should give him the honour.'

Almond opened his mouth, then closed it again.

'We are going,' the lanista said, suddenly. 'I will no longer hide from our past problems.'

'Are you sure this is a good idea?' Erik said, worry etched on his face.

The lanista laid a hand on Erik's shoulder. 'We shall hide no longer. Let's go to Battleacre and give our gladiators the chance to earn their freedom. Let's show the amphitheatre crowds who Ludus Capri really is.'

The next morning, Almond followed the crowd of gladiators and servants into the courtyard.

'You are travelling next to Hans,' Erik said, pointing Almond to where the champion gladiator stood.

‘Where is Scrappy?’ Almond said.

‘Mahina is going to look after him while we are away,’ Erik said.

‘I am not leaving my dog.’ Almond stepped out of the line.

A guard stepped forward and aimed his spear at Almond.

‘Get back in line, servant,’ Erik said. ‘Your dog will be safe here.’

‘Of course I am coming, Father,’ Mahina said, walking out into the courtyard. ‘And so is Jarod.’

‘I forbid it,’ the lanista said, walking in behind her. ‘You shall stay here and take care of our household.’

The corner of Almond’s mouth broke into a smile as he saw Scrappy cradled in her arms.

‘I am coming and that is the end of it,’ Mahina said, moving to the front gate. ‘The carriage is outside and ready for us.’

The lanista looked up at the sky and let out a long sigh. ‘Don’t make me regret this, Mahina.’

The front gate opened with a loud screech. Scrappy’s ears lay flat against his head. A carriage with four horses waited on the road. Mahina walked out of the gate and climbed through the carriage door Jarod held open.

Almond stepped into line next to Hans.

The lanista walked out of the estate and climbed onto a large black horse. Erik waited as a guard brought a second black horse around for him.

Erik climbed on, checked everyone was ready, then shouted. ‘Move out!’

A crack of a whip sounded through the courtyard. The horses went first, followed by the carriage, and then the line of gladiators and servants, with guards walking casually alongside them.

‘Why doesn’t anyone try to escape?’ Almond said, looking up at Hans.

Hans raised an eyebrow. ‘Why would we want to escape? We

are going to the famous Battleacre. We get to fight for our freedom.'

'You could just fight here and earn your freedom,' Almond said.

'You have no honour,' Hans said, spitting into the ground. 'Only a dog would kill a lesser opponent, then run.'

Almond gave Hans a smile. 'I am surprised there are still people with such honour.'

'Have you any honour, little man?' Hans said. 'Will you fight beside me in Battleacre's great arena?'

'I think you should find another servant,' Almond said, looking away. 'I promised someone I wouldn't fight.'

'You will fight, servant,' Hans said, looking at Almond with a wide smile. 'The warrior in you will rise again. I can sense it.'

Almond ignored Hans and lifted his head to get a view of the cart.

'I shall tell you if I see or hear anything about your precious dog,' Hans said.

Almond gave the massive warrior a thank-you nod.

The caravan of gladiators and servants followed the winding path down through the small valley and out into an open plain. They joined the cobblestone road and continued west with the sun in their eyes. Servants walked up and down the caravan, handing out skins of water and dried meats. A few hours later, the first rolling hills of the eastern horse lands appeared. They went down the first hill and up the other side.

'Look,' Hans said, pointing into the distance. 'Aren't they beautiful?'

A herd of horses sprinted down a hill, up the other side, and over the crest of the next one.

'We should reach the famous horse farms by sundown,' Hans said.

'I don't see many horses near where I live,' Almond said. 'It seems the far south is not the friendliest anymore.'

Hans looked down at Almond in surprise. 'You lived in the far south? That is beast country. I am surprised you are still alive.'

'Scrappy is my alarm,' Almond said, peering at the cart again. 'He went crazy anytime he caught a beast's scent.'

Hans nodded his approval. 'Man's best friend.'

They reached the bottom of the next rolling hill and began the long climb up to the crest. The sun, now to their right, was halfway on its journey to the horizon. They reached the top of the hill, then began the long walk down the next.

'See the filtering smoke over there?' Hans said, pointing to the crest of the next hill. 'Those are the horse farms ahead.'

'It seems you have a love for horses, Hans.'

He smiled. 'I wish to be a horseman in the Queen's military. It is one of the most honourable positions.'

'A horseman?' Almond said. 'I would have thought you would want to be in the Queen's Guard or become a Queen's assassin?'

'Knife slingers.' Hans spat at the ground. 'Formidable warriors, but they have no honour.'

Almond raised both of his eyebrows. 'Are you sure about that?'

'I have met one in my lifetime,' Hans said. 'He was a drunk, boorish man who spoke down to everyone.'

At the bottom of the hill, the caravan slowed slightly as Erik rode his horse up the incline. He disappeared over the crest just as the lanista called the caravan to a halt.

'Don't want to surprise the horsemen now, do we?' Hans said. 'I wouldn't like to see a full cavalry come over that hill.'

The caravan waited in silence. After half an hour, a sense of nervousness rippled through the gladiators and servants. The sun dipped past the crest of the rolling hill and dusk set in. Erik appeared at the top of the hill and waved. The lanista waved his hand forward.

'Mr Erik must have negotiated hard if he was there for that long,' Hans said. 'I feel any homestead would be cautious with this many gladiators and servants on its doorstep.'

They reached the top of the hill and walked onto the large plains of the horse farms. Massive fenced fields housed hundreds of horses of all shapes and sizes. At the end of each field stood a house with woodsmoke pouring out of the chimney next to a long stable with high doors.

'Do we stop here for the night?' Almond said.

'There are fields at the end of the horse farms where we will set up camp. Erik will replenish supplies for the long walk tomorrow.'

Almond scanned the fields as they walked through the horse farms. Horses called to each other, creating a sing-song of neighs and nickers. As they walked in between the fields, the horses bobbed their heads in greeting. The last field they came to was devoid of any horses. Blackened firepits were dotted around the field where previous travellers had camped. Erik signalled to the guards, who walked up to the furthest firepit and made a wide circle. The gladiators and servants walked into the area and sat near the large pit. Servants fanned out and collected wood to start up a roaring fire.

'Almond,' Jarod said, skipping into the area. 'Pascal has asked you to come to the cart.'

Erik signalled to a guard who strode over to Almond's shoulder.

'Is Scrappy OK?' Almond said, following Jarod to the carriage.

Jarod smiled over his shoulder. 'He is awake. Pascal said he will be up and about in a day.'

Almond let out a long sigh.

'Hello,' Mahina said, stepping out of the carriage. 'Jarod says your name is Almond.'

'Yes, Almond is correct.'

'Your dog is looking for you,' Mahina said with a smile. 'We cannot bring him outside yet as he is still recovering.'

'I am not permitted to let him into the carriage, my lady,' the guard said, indicating Almond.

Mahina pursed a lip. 'What if you cuff him and escort him in?'

The guard paused for a second. 'Can you get permission from Sir Erik, my lady?'

'Go and ask Erik please, Jarod,' Mahina said.

Jarod darted off through the sitting servants and gladiators.

'My father says you are a warrior?' Mahina said.

Almond smiled. 'Another lifetime, my lady.'

'You may have to use your skills in this lifetime,' Mahina said. 'For the sake of your dog.'

Almond played with his medallion. 'We will see, my lady.'

'My father was once a gladiator,' Mahina said. 'You would do well to listen to him.'

Almond looked at Mahina with raised eyebrows. 'And he earned his freedom?'

'He did. He wanted to be in the Queen's Guard but fell in love with my mother,' Mahina said, with a flicker of sadness. 'He's a good man.'

'I am sorry about your mother,' Almond said, blinking.

'How do you know what happened to my mother?' Mahina said.

'I didn't,' Almond said, with a tilt of his head. 'Until your face betrayed you.'

'I never really knew her,' Mahina said. 'I was too young.'

Erik and Jarod appeared from the darkness.

'You have but a few moments to see your pet,' Erik said. 'Mahina, you will stay here.'

Mahina opened her mouth, then thought better of saying something. She walked over to Erik and stood by his side. The guard entered the carriage. Erik waved Almond forward.

Almond entered the carriage and dropped to a knee. Scrappy's tail thumped hard against the makeshift bed.

'I thought I had lost you, little one,' Almond said, placing his forehead next to Scrappy's. Scrappy looked up with sad brown eyes, as if asking for forgiveness.

'Silly dog,' Almond said, wiping a tear from his cheek. 'You did nothing wrong.'

'Out you get,' Pascal said, appearing from the darkness. 'Your dog needs some rest.'

Almond rubbed Scrappy's ear one last time, then exited the carriage. Scrappy, too tired to look back, placed his head on the soft bed and closed his eyes.

'I cannot thank you enough, Medicus,' Almond said. 'I will be forever grateful.'

Pascal grumbled something about pets under his breath, then disappeared into the carriage. The guard exited and led Almond to where Erik stood.

'Get your rest,' Erik said. 'Tomorrow, we walk a full day and half a night.'

'Thank you,' Almond said to Mahina, Jarod and Erik, before walking off to find Hans.

After Almond navigated the group of gladiators, he found Hans sitting with his feet inches from the fire.

'How is your puppy?' he said.

'He will survive,' Almond said.

'Then you must make sure you survive for your pet,' Hans said. 'Sleep over there.'

Almond walked over to where Hans pointed. He rolled up into a ball, closed his eyes, and went to sleep.

CHAPTER 3
TWO SHORT SWORDS

The carriage wheels squeaked to life as four horses strained to get it moving. Almond yawned while rubbing the sleep out of his eyes. The first sign of the sun's glow appeared in the east. With all the horses in their stables, the farms looked empty and forlorn compared with the previous day. Eventually, the carriage cleared the last farm and joined the road east.

'Are you up for this, warrior?' Hans said, looking down at Almond. 'We have a long way to go.'

'Stop calling me warrior,' Almond said, shaking his head. 'One-and-a-half days of travel isn't too long. Scrappy and I have done longer.'

'We turn north after the second bridge, then continue through the rolling hills to the magnificent city of Battleacre,' Hans said, puffing out his chest.

Almond smiled at the big man's enthusiasm.

The caravan moved slowly along the east road towards the main road north. As the sun crested the top of the sky, the horses' metal shoes sounded over the first bridge. They continued along the road for a few more hours until they crossed the second bridge. Erik called a halt and directed the caravan to form a circle. Once formed, Jarod and the servants moved around the camp, handing out food and water.

'We move north now,' Hans said, peering at the distant rolling hills. 'The hills get particularly steep from here on in.'

'What about the horses?' Almond said. 'Are they able to keep going?'

'Battleacre horse couriers will meet us halfway. We will swap our horses for new ones then continue north,' Hans said. 'We need to keep going so we can reach Battleacre before the games begin.'

After finishing their food, the caravan continued the trek north. Several hills later, Almond watched the sun disappear over the western horizon. He dragged his hand across his brow to stop sweat falling into his eyes. Suddenly, the caravan came to a halt.

'What is going on?' Almond said, standing on his toes.

'It looks like a servant has fallen,' Hans said. 'Collapsed from the long walk.'

Almond stepped out of the line to get a better look. Guards moved in and surrounded a small man who lay face-first on the ground.

'Get back in line,' a guard said, poking Almond in the back.

'What are they going to do with him?' Almond said. 'Get the medicus to come and help him.'

Hans grabbed Almond and pulled him into line. 'What happens to the servant is the gladiator's choice. Never get involved in another gladiator's business.'

'What do you mean?' Almond said, confused. 'The gladiator doesn't own him?'

'He doesn't, but a gladiator's servant is under the ward of the gladiator,' Hans said. 'As you are my ward, I choose what happens to you when I want to.'

'You what?' Almond said, his mouth dropping open.

Hans chuckled. 'We are both slaves, little man, but you more than I. Get in line and behave yourself.'

A moment later, a stocky man hoisted an unconscious servant over his shoulder.

'It seems the gladiator has taken a shine to his servant,' Hans said, smiling down at Almond.

Almond folded his arms and looked away. Hans let out another deep-throated chuckle. A whistle sent the carriage jerking forward, and the caravan continued its walk up the hill. A few hours later, the caravan reached a campsite where they shared food and water and swapped the horses with fresh ones brought from Battleacre stables.

'We are close,' Hans said, raising his chin to the north. 'We have a few more hills and then an open plain where we will see the magnificent city.'

The caravan left the campsite and continued over the hills. The air chilled with the sun's absence. In the distance, the long, mournful howls of wolves bounced through the hills.

'There,' Hans said, a little too loudly. 'Can you see that?'

Almond squinted. 'I can't see anything. No wait. I can. A light!'

A small light just over the crest of the hill blinked.

'It is at the top of the arena,' Hans said. 'We have made it to Battleacre.'

They reached the crest of the hill and entered a wide, flat plain. Up ahead, the city of Battleacre loomed. Almond wrapped his arms around himself and shivered.

'Are you nervous, servant?' Hans said. 'We earn our freedom or die in the next few days. Our destiny.'

'It is called Battleacre for a reason, Hans. It is a place of death,' Almond said. 'Of course I am nervous.'

The carriage reached the southern gate, where it came to a halt.

Guards from the city walked along the caravan, looking everyone up and down. As the guards walked past Almond, he bowed his head and stared at his shoes.

Hans frowned down at his servant. 'Looks like you are hiding something, servant. What is going on?'

Almond kept his head lowered.

'Come on,' Hans said. 'Tell me what is going on.'

Once all the guards had passed, Almond looked up at Hans. 'Nothing is going on, Hans. I just don't like people seeing who I am.'

Hans snorted. 'I somehow don't believe you.'

When the guards reached the end of the caravan, they signalled at the gate to let them pass. At the gate, two guards waved the carriage through.

Almond groaned at the throng of people filling the four cobbled lanes of the north–south road. When Battleacre citizens saw the group of gladiators advancing, they hurried to the side of the street to get out of the way and watch the fighting men walk past.

'Magnificent, isn't it?' Hans said, moving his hand in a wide arc. 'We will fight with vigour and honour, servant.'

Almond still kept his head bowed. 'If you say so, Hans. I prefer the outside world where I can be at one with nature.'

'And beasts around every corner who would love to do nothing more than kill you and eat you,' Hans said, shaking his head.

The carriage wound up the wide road until it reached a square.

'This is the southern gate,' Hans said as they moved in. 'We are going around the west side of the arena and down into the hypogeum.'

Almond pulled his collar around his neck before raising his head. He took in a deep breath of Battleacre's familiar smells.

'I knew it,' Hans said. 'You have been here before, haven't you?'

'I have,' Almond said. 'And it would be a good idea to keep that to yourself.'

Hans held up a hand. 'I am here to fight and earn my honour. I have no quarrel with your past. But I would like you to be honest with me, so I know I have someone who will stand with me.'

'I will stand with you, Hans,' Almond said, scanning the high walls of the arena and noting the flags on the arena roof.

The train passed the southern square, then turned north up the amphitheatre's western side. Halfway along, Erik brought the train to a halt.

Almond watched the carriage continue north, then turn left. 'Where are they going?'

'I would think the lanista and his family won't stay in the arena,' Hans said.

'They have gone into the entertainment district,' Almond said.

To their right, a large wrought-iron gate clacked open. Rays of sunlight shone down a long ramp that disappeared underneath the arena. The lanista's magistrus pointed down the ramp, signalling for the gladiators to descend. A roar sounded from the arena above them.

'To the hypogeum we descend,' Hans said, slamming his hand against his chest.

'Hans,' a large man shouted. 'You finally made it to Battleacre. How did your lanista afford it? Did he sell his daughter?'

A group of men burst into laughter.

Hans spun around and snarled at the group of men standing to one side of the long ramp. 'I will see you in the arena, Gron,' he said. 'And this time I will send you to your maker.'

Gron raised his head, sneered, and dragged his thumb across his throat. 'You will be a dead man before tomorrow night, old man. You have no place in this famous amphitheatre.'

Hans spat on the ground. 'Ludus Capri always has a place.'

'Let's get out of here,' Almond said, grabbing Hans by the

forearm. 'You don't want to be removed from the tournament before it even starts.'

An almighty roar sounded from above. Hans tore his eyes off Gron and strode off down the ramp and into the dimly lit hypogeum. They caught up to the lanista's group of gladiators and servants and fell in behind. A few more twists and turns later, and they entered a large caged room.

'This is our home for the tournament,' the magistrus said. 'We represent the Ludus Capri, the lanista's house. We shall keep this place tidy and respect this great city and its games.'

The gladiators and servants shouted the Ludus Capri battle call before each of them found a spot on the floor, where they stretched out their blankets.

'Be ready at all times,' the magistrus said. 'Your name can be called at any time.'

Almond sat down and leant back against one of the cage's bars. He took in a deep breath, then brought his knees up to his chest.

'Are you going to tell me what is going on?' Hans said, throwing a cloth at Almond. 'You are sweating and it's not that hot.'

Almond grabbed the cloth and wiped the sweat from his brow. 'This place brings back bad memories. I do not wish to be here.'

'Get some rest, slave,' the magistrus said. 'Tomorrow is going to be a long day.'

A round of trumpets sounded from the top. To the right of the Ludus Capri's cage, a ramp led to a large wooden door. The door swung open, letting in a stream of sunlight. The sound of the crowd in the arena roared through the doorway.

A man walked down the ramp and handed a piece of paper to a

runner. The runner ran off down through the caged rooms. A moment later, a gladiator and his servant ran past.

'Have you given the magistrus your list of favourite weapons?' Hans said, raising an eyebrow at Almond.

'What do you mean, my favourite weapon?' Almond said, pulling on his sandals.

Hans gave Almond a look of confusion. 'I know you have been here before, servant. You know exactly what I am talking about.'

Almond frowned. 'I have no clue what you are talking about, Hans. And how about you start using my name?'

A flash of anger streaked through Hans's face. A moment later, though, his face softened with realisation. 'They must have implemented the arena's new rules after you were here, then.'

Almond scratched the side of his head. 'What new rules?'

Hans guided Almond out of the cage and to the arena wall's long, thin viewing window. 'Let me show you.'

Almond stepped on a concrete brick that lifted him to the same height as Hans.

'There are four quadrants. On the wall of each quadrant, there are five panels. Four at the bottom and one at the top. In the bottom four panels, there are random weapons. Your favourite weapon is in the top panel.'

Almond scanned the walls and located the five panels. A trumpet sound reverberated through the arena. Four gladiators and their servants walked to the middle. They all turned to the podium and bowed. The games announcer listed each ludus and its colours. Once finished, the gladiators retreated into their quadrants.

'That is the General,' Hans said, pointing to a man sitting high above the podium. 'It is where he sits with his family and the mayor's family. The people below the General are members of the council.'

'Why the colours on the gladiators?' Almond said.

'The colours of the elements,' Hans said. 'Red, blue, yellow and green. They represent the gods of old. They assigned each ludus a colour.'

A man walked up to an oversized alphorn sitting next to the podium. He waited a second, then sent a massive ear-ringing blast through the amphitheatre.

The crowd roared and stamped their feet.

The fighting gladiators and servants reached into the first panel and grabbed their weapons. Most looked at their weapons with complete disgust.

'Why don't they just take their favourite weapon?' Almond said.

'It is about survival,' Hans said. 'Survival and honour. If you retrieve your favourite weapons, the rest of the gladiators will target you.'

'And even with your favourite weapon, you will not survive that,' Almond said.

'Only a warrior would know that,' Hans said, nudging Almond. 'Are your fighting instincts returning?'

Almond massaged the medallion hanging from his neck. 'I vowed I would never fight another man in anger again. You are asking too much of me, Hans.'

Hans's eyes softened. He turned back to the fight. 'When there are only two gladiators left, they can get their favourite weapon. But if they get disarmed, they cannot go back for the other weapons.'

'Certain death,' Almond said.

'Yes, certain death, but an honourable death,' Hans said, placing his hand on his chest. 'Are you ready to fight by my side? Even though I ask too much.'

Almond lowered his head. 'I swore, Hans. I swore on my loved ones' graves.'

'What of your pet dog?' Hans said. 'Is he not worth fighting for?'

Almond looked up at Hans. 'You will use my best friend against me?'

Hans held up a hand. 'I am just telling you that your pet will not have an owner if you are not around anymore. It is just a fact. The world is not a friendly place.'

After a few minutes spent watching the fighting, Almond turned to Hans. 'I will fight, but you are to tell nobody of my past. If you do, I shall forfeit and you will lose, too.'

A wide smile stretched across Hans's face. 'I shall tell nobody. We shall use this to our advantage.'

'And I am to be guaranteed both mine and Scrappy's freedom,' Almond said.

'You know I cannot guarantee that,' Hans said. 'I am a slave as much as you are.'

'You have influence,' Almond said. 'You are the lanista's champion.'

Hans turned and searched the room. 'I will speak to Erik and see if he will entertain it.'

The crowd in the amphitheatre hushed. Almond looked out of the window just in time to see a gladiator dispatch a fallen gladiator's servant.

'That gladiator has no honour,' Hans said. 'His servant is still alive. He should have let him fight the servant of the fallen gladiator.'

A single boo from the crowd broke the silence. Another boo answered the first one. A moment later, the entire amphitheatre's crowd booed the gladiator. He lifted his head and shouted obscenities at the crowd. The remaining two gladiators and their servants rounded on their disgraced competitor.

'He will not live long,' Hans said, resting his forearms on the windowsill. 'If you fight with dishonour, they will target you.'

Almond watched the two gladiators drive the single gladiator into his own quadrant. They toyed with him, playing to the roaring, cheering crowd. One gladiator's servant sneaked up behind the disgraced gladiator and drove a short sword through him. The gladiator fell face-first into the soft brown sand of the arena. The two remaining gladiators sprinted to their quadrants and retrieved their favourite weapons from the top panel.

'That gladiator still had weapons left in the other panels,' Almond said.

'Not a good idea taking on a gladiator who has his favourite weapon,' Hans said.

Almond nodded. 'Certain death.'

'Remember, the other gladiator doesn't have to wait while you retrieve your weapon,' Hans said. 'If you take your time, he can cut you off from getting your weapon.'

Almond watched the two gladiators meet with an almighty crash in the middle of the arena. He jumped as Jarod appeared next to him.

'Mr Almond,' Jarod said. 'We have a surprise for you.'

'You scared me,' Almond said, turning around. 'Mahina. Scrappy!'

The little dog nestling in Mahina's arms thumped his tail hard.

'Dogs not allowed down here,' the magistrus grumbled from inside the Ludus Capri cage.

'I am sure you can ignore this for your favourite gladiator and his servant?' Mahina said, smiling.

The magistrus snorted, then turned and continued talking to the other gladiators.

Mahina lowered Scrappy to the ground.

The little dog hobbled over to Almond. 'Silly dog,' Almond said, playing with his ears. 'I thought I had lost you forever.'

Scrappy licked Almond's hand, then whined at the noise inside the arena.

'Can probably smell the other animals,' Hans said. 'Would be good to keep this tiny dog out of the arena.'

'I will continue looking after him for you,' Mahina said.

'What if we don't win?' Almond said.

Hans slapped Almond on the back. 'What do you mean? Of course we are going to win!'

'I will look after him,' Jarod said. 'That is a promise, Mr Almond. I will look after him.'

'You best ask Mahina first, Jarod,' Almond said. 'I don't think servants are allowed to keep dogs.'

'It will be fine,' Mahina said. 'I will keep him safe.'

'Hans!' the magistrus shouted. 'Your number is up!'

'What are your favourite weapons?' Hans hissed. 'Tell me quickly.'

'Two short swords,' Almond said, giving Scrappy a last pet.

Mahina leant in so only Almond and Hans could hear. 'I need you to come and see me after your fight.'

Almond opened his mouth, but Mahina had already turned and made for the corridors.

The wooden door opened. Almond squinted at the sun streaming through the doorway.

Hans puffed his chest out, slammed his fist against his breast, and looked down at Almond. 'Are you ready, servant?'

Almond reached for the small chain around his neck. He pulled up the little medallion and kissed it. 'Forgive me,' he whispered.

'Ludus Capri is represented by the earth element,' Hans said. 'The lanista's house is of earth's origin. We shall fight for his honour.'

'And his wealth,' Almond muttered.

They reached the arena's centre and faced the podium. Almond scanned the other contestants. All three servants were a foot taller than himself. A trumpet sounded. The gamekeeper read out the details of each house, then turned and looked at the General. A nod of the head and the keeper gave the signal. Hans and Almond ran to the earth quarter where they watched and waited. The gamekeeper walked up to the alphorn and gave it a single long blast. The first of the panels slammed open. Hans reached in and pulled out a dagger. Almond reached in and pulled out a long pole.

'Swap?' Almond said, raising both eyebrows.

Hans flipped over the dagger and offered it to Almond. Just as Almond grabbed the dagger, an arrow slammed into the wall next to him.

'Coward weapon,' Hans shouted. 'I will have your head.'

Across the arena, a servant hopped from foot to foot while cackling with glee.

Hans sprinted forward and met the gladiators in the centre with an almighty crunch.

Almond scanned the arena and kept a firm eye on the other three servants. A gladiator's weapon went flying. The servant and the gladiator retrieved their second set of surprise weapons.

Hans fought with precision and agility for such a big man. Almond warded off the other servants who tried to get him from behind.

'Next weapon,' Hans hollered, running past Almond.

Almond dropped the knife and turned straight into another servant.

'Shouldn't have dropped that,' the servant said, jabbing a sword at him.

Almond sidestepped the sword, took a step forward, and slammed the heel of his hand through the servant's nose. The servant fell to his knees. Almond ran for the panels in his quadrant.

'So much for you keeping your fighting skills quiet,' Hans said, his mouth hanging open. 'They will target you from now on.'

Out came a small hammer from the panel.

'If it means getting Scrappy out of this place, I will fight,' Almond said.

Hans took off back into the fray. Almond jogged after him, but slowed before he got to the centre. A gladiator broke away from the centre and charged him. Almond sidestepped, then ran until he reached the arena wall. There, he kept the wall to his left as he ran the length of the arena. A thud sounded behind him as a weapon hit the wooden wall. Almond sprinted faster.

Hans shouted expletives as he caught sight of the gladiator and the servant chasing Almond around the arena. With an almighty battle-cry, Hans took off at a sprint. A second later, the chasing gladiator slammed into the arena wall. Hans reached down, grabbed him by the hair, then ran him through with his weapon.

'You are on your own now,' Almond said, spinning around and facing the servant.

The servant stopped and stared at Almond.

Almond walked forward with his small hammer raised.

The servant dropped his weapon and fell to his knees.

'Kill, kill, kill,' the crowd chanted.

Almond looked up into the crowd, sneered, and gave them a rude signal. After a brief silence, the crowd roared their approval. The servant got up and ran towards the closed wooden doors. The doors cracked open, and they let him through.

Almond ran back to the earth quadrant where Hans was reaching into the fifth panel. 'Only two gladiators left,' Hans said, dragging out a scimitar. Its blade curved to a vicious point. Almond reached in and pulled out two rusted short swords.

'Someone will pay,' Hans said, looking at the swords. 'I have a feeling Gron has something to do with that.'

The other gladiator and his servant stood ready in the middle.

'Remember, they are proficient with their weapons,' Hans said.

'So are we,' Almond said, weighing his swords.

They charged at the gladiator, but before they could get there, the gladiator dropped to his knees. Blood trickled out of his mouth. With a thud, he fell face-first into the dirt. Behind him, his servant stood with a long, blood-soaked spear.

Almond looked at Hans. 'What now?'

'You have to fight him now,' Hans said, backing away.

The servant dropped the knife and fell to his knees. 'I will not fight.'

Almond looked up at the expectant crowd.

'Kill, kill, kill,' the crowd chanted.

Almond walked back to where Hans stood.

'What are you doing?' Hans said. 'You need to fight him.'

'I am not fighting a man who throws down his weapon,' Almond said, while watching the servant make his way back to the wooden doors.

'He will not survive his lanista's wrath,' Hans said. 'He murdered his own gladiator.'

The gamekeeper walked to the end of the podium. He pulled the earth flag from its holder and waved it, signalling the winning team. Hans raised his hand and took in the adoration of the screaming, cheering crowd. Almond waited for him to finish, then followed him back through the wooden doors and into their cell.

The lanista walked up and extended a hand to Hans. 'A well-fought match.'

Hans grabbed the lanista's forearm. 'For Ludus Capri, sir.'

'You lied to me,' the lanista said, smiling at Almond. 'I should punish you for not telling the truth.'

Almond shrugged. 'My past is my own, sir.'

Hans slapped Almond on the back. 'Come on, winner. We must eat and save our energy. We have a long tournament.'

'My daughter has asked that you visit,' the lanista said to Almond. 'You and Hans will come to the carriage. Erik will come and fetch you and my guards will escort you.'

Almond bowed. 'I thank you, sir.'

'Food,' Hans hollered.

Jarod and a few other servants walked into the room holding trays of cooked meats and bread.

Hans grabbed a plate and piled it as high as it could go.

Almond followed Hans to the back of the cell and sat with his back against the bars.

'You don't eat much,' Hans said, sliding down next to Almond.

'Not as big as you, see?' Almond said, looking the big man over.

Hans chuckled, then shoved as much food as he could into his mouth.

'Slave,' a man called from the other side of the cell. 'I know you, slave.'

Almond turned and narrowed his eyes. On the other side of the bars stood a thin-faced man.

'Who are you and what do you want?' the magistrus said. 'This cell is reserved for Ludus Capri.'

The thin-faced man smiled warmly. 'I knew we would find you one day, Almond.'

'Who is he?' Hans said, nudging Almond with his elbow.

Almond dumped his plate of food to one side. 'He is a nobody. Someone from my past. Ignore him.'

'Your brothers want you back, Almond,' the man said. 'You have jobs to finish.'

The magistrus marched towards the thin-faced man.

'Stop, magistrus,' Almond shouted.

The magistrus stopped and turned with an eyebrow raised. 'You will speak to your magistrus in this way?'

Almond stood and walked over to him. 'Go away, Dimitri. You are not welcome here.'

Dimitri chuckled.

'Get away from our room,' the magistrus thundered.

'We will see each other shortly, Almond,' Dimitri said, waving a hand before disappearing into the shadows.

The magistrus faced Almond. 'Who is he?'

Almond kept his mouth shut.

‘It would be good if you told us, Almond,’ Hans said, walking up behind them. ‘So we know what we are dealing with?’

‘He won’t bother us again,’ Almond said. ‘Let us please drop this.’

The gate to their quarters opened and in walked Erik. ‘Time to visit Mahina—’ he said, pulling up short. ‘What is going on here?’

‘It seems your servant has history here in Battleacre,’ the magistrus said. ‘He just had a visitor.’

Erik looked at Almond. ‘We will discuss this on the way to the entertainment district. Follow me.’

‘You two,’ the magistrus said. ‘Do not let them out of your sight.’

Two guards walked up and towered over Almond.

‘Let us move,’ Erik said. ‘The sun is starting to set.’

Almond and Hans followed Erik through the hypogeum until they reached the ramp to the western gate. As they ascended, the two guards walked closer to Almond, their hands on their swords. The wrought-iron gate clacked open. The burning firepits of the blacksmiths district shone brightly.

‘Stick close by, Almond,’ Erik said, walking north. ‘The entertainment district is up ahead on the left. We need to make our way to the lanista’s carriage.’

They turned left into a wide street filled on either side with bars and restaurants. People filtered in and out of the establishments in different states of alcohol-induced revelry. The big western wall of Battleacre loomed far up ahead.

‘Keep moving,’ Erik muttered as they dodged between the singing, drunk people. ‘When we get close to the wall, we turn right into the camp area and walk to the back.’

Just before the wall, they turned right into a campsite filled with luxurious carriages. At the back of the campsite, the lanista’s small carriage stood completely out of place.

'Almond,' Jarod said, walking from behind the carriage. 'You made it. Little Scrappy is waiting for you.'

Erik halted the guards, then looked at Almond. 'Be warned that any attempt at escape will end your life, the dog's life and Jarod's life.'

'I understand,' Almond said, walking to the carriage.

Jarod knocked lightly on the door.

The door swung open and Mahina poked out her head. 'You made it. Come on in,' she said. 'Scrappy will be glad to see you.'

Almond stepped into the carriage and grinned as Scrappy greeted him, licking his face.

'Close the door please, Jarod,' Mahina said.

'Won't Erik be upset?' Almond said as the door closed.

Mahina lowered her voice. 'I need to speak to you urgently.'

Almond raised an eyebrow. 'About?'

Mahina sat forward. 'A thin-faced man came to see me in the dead of night. He told me the General's son is in danger and that you can help.'

'Dimitri,' Almond said, his voice lowering. 'You should not trust what he says.'

Mahina sat back. 'He said you would say that. He said Ludus Leo is going to capture the General's son. Dimitri needs your help.'

'Is everything OK in there, Mahina?' Erik said from outside the carriage.

'Everything is fine, Erik,' Mahina shouted. 'Let Almond enjoy time with his dog.'

Erik muttered something from the other side of the door.

'I don't know how I can help,' Almond said. 'I am caged and must fight in the arena.'

'It is all I know,' Mahina said, spreading her hands.

Almond continued to play with Scrappy while he sat deep in thought.

A tap sounded on the door.

'You must go,' Mahina said. 'You must help Dimitri. I cannot let any harm come to the General's son.'

'You two are together?' Almond said.

Mahina turned a light pink. 'Please help Dimitri.'

With a long sigh, Almond looked down at Scrappy. 'This is an area of my life I do not wish to go back to,' he said. 'I will speak to Dimitri but only once.'

'Thank you,' Mahina said with a small sigh.

Almond stroked Scrappy's head. 'Take good care of this young lady, you hear?'

Scrappy barked once.

The carriage door swung open. 'Everything OK?' Erik said, looking at Mahina.

'Everything is OK, thank you, Erik,' Mahina said.

Almond climbed out of the carriage and walked over to Hans. After Erik had finished speaking to Mahina, they left the campsite and made their way through the entertainment district. Revellers cheered as they noticed Hans walking past. Some complained that the slave should be in a cage.

Just before they turned onto the north–south street, Almond caught a flash of movement. He stopped walking. A guard pressed him on the shoulder.

'What is it?' Erik said.

Almond spun and searched the crowd with narrow eyes. 'Mahina,' he said. 'Get the guards back to Mahina now, Erik!'

'What for?' Erik said. 'What did you see?'

'He is playing us for a fool,' one guard said.

'Get them back to Mahina. Now!' Almond shouted.

'Both of you, go!' Erik said. 'Get back to the carriage.'

The guards hesitated.

'Now!' Erik shouted.

CHAPTER 4

A HOODED FIGURE

Almond, Hans and Erik reached the carriage moments after the guards. The two guards lay face-down in the dirt.

Erik ripped the carriage door open. 'Nobody. They are gone. Mahina, Jarod, your dog, all gone.'

Almond knelt next to one guard. He pulled away his coat to see long, thin cuts across his chest.

'Do you know who did this?' Hans said, kneeling next to Almond.

'I may have a suspect,' Almond said quietly. 'Only certain warriors inflict these types of wounds.'

Erik bent over and grabbed Almond by the scruff of the neck. 'I suggest you talk. The lanista will show no mercy when his daughter is involved.'

'Take it easy, Erik,' Hans said. 'He is on our side.'

'They are part of the Queen's Guard,' Almond said, shrugging Erik's hand off. 'The knife slingers.'

'And why would they have taken Mahina?' Erik said, folding his arms.

Almond opened his mouth, then closed it. 'This cannot be right. There is something wrong here.'

'What are you thinking?' Hans said.

'I do not want to give the lanista bad news about his daughter,' Erik said, worry etched on his face.

'The knife slingers are honourable,' Almond said. 'Somebody else is doing this and making it look like them. Does the lanista have any enemies who want to see him suffer?'

'Every lanista has enemies,' Erik said. 'And in particular, lanistae that were once gladiators and have earned their freedom.'

'Hold on,' Hans said, raising a hand. 'Did you hear that?'

Almond, Hans and Erik all tilted their heads.

'It's coming from behind the carriage,' Almond said.

'A wild animal.' Hans crouched and grabbed a guard's sword.

Almond walked slowly around the carriage. 'Scrappy. It's Scrappy.'

'Sword please, Hans,' Erik said, holding out his hand.

Hans smiled and dropped the sword.

'Did you see anything, little one?' Almond said. 'Where are Mahina and Jarod?'

Scrappy growled, then licked Almond's face.

'Do you think he can help us?' Erik said. 'I mean, can he sniff out where they went?'

'Get me something of Mahina and Jarod's,' Almond said, pointing his chin at the carriage.

Erik retrieved an item of clothing from each.

'Here you go, boy,' Almond said, letting Scrappy sniff the clothes. 'Can you find any of them?'

Almond lowered Scrappy to the ground and watched the little dog sniff around the carriage. A few moments later, he hobbled towards the main road of the entertainment district.

'He has caught a scent,' Almond said, walking after Scrappy. 'Which one, I don't know.'

They turned left onto the main road and walked towards the

entertainment district. Singing, shouts and screams came out of the bars and restaurants.

Scrappy suddenly stopped. He walked in circles, sniffing the ground.

'I think he has lost the scent,' Almond said, kneeling.

Scrappy circled again and let out a whine.

Almond scooped Scrappy up into his arms. 'It's OK, little one.'

'Where do we go?' Hans said.

'We check the alleys,' Almond said. 'They do most of the black-market dealings inside them.'

'You definitely know this town a lot better than you are letting on,' Hans said.

Almond walked up to Erik and held out Scrappy. 'Can you look after him?'

'I don't want to look after your dog.' Erik frowned.

'It's insurance,' Almond said. 'Now you know I won't run away.'

Erik let out a sigh and took the small dog.

'Let's go, servant,' Hans said.

They made their way down the first alley. Shady characters pulled their hoods over their heads. Some disappeared into doorways. Some disappeared down other alleys.

The second alley was no different. Every time they approached someone, they would cover themselves up or disappear down another alley.

'Enough of this,' Hans said, walking up to a man and grabbing him by the scruff of the neck. 'Have you seen a girl and a boy around here?'

The man stared wide-eyed at Hans.

'Answer me,' Hans said, shaking him. 'Have you seen a girl and a boy?'

With his eyes closed, the man shook his head vigorously.

'Let's try another alley,' Almond said, walking back to the main street.

Hans dropped the man and followed Almond. They turned down the third alley but were greeted with more blank stares or fearful ramblings.

Almond turned down the fourth alley. 'Jarod,' he said, rushing down the alley. 'Hans, get over here.'

Hans jogged over and knelt. 'Is he alive?'

Almond placed his ear on Jarod's chest. He coughed.

'Mahina,' Jarod said. 'They have Mahina.'

'Who are they?' Almond said. 'Who has the girl, Jarod?'

'The thin-faced man,' Jarod said. 'He has her.'

Hans frowned at Almond. 'So, it was him.'

'It makes little sense,' Almond said. 'The knife slingers wouldn't do something so dishonourable.'

'No, no,' Jarod said. 'The thin-faced man saved us.'

Almond moved in closer. 'He saved you from who?'

'We need to get him to the medicus,' Hans said. 'He doesn't look good, Almond.'

'We need to know who was after her,' Almond said.

'I will carry him,' Hans said. 'Ask your questions on the way.'

Jarod groaned as Hans picked him up and placed him on his shoulder.

'Who was after Mahina, Jarod?' Almond said.

'Oh my,' Erik said, seeing them come out of the alley. 'Is that the boy?'

Hans nodded.

'Who has Mahina, Jarod,' Almond said. 'Speak to me.'

'Assassins,' Jarod said, coughing loudly. 'The thin-faced man said assassins are after her.'

'Who killed the guards?' Almond said.

Jarod coughed again, then cleared his throat. 'It was the thin-faced man. The guards attacked him when he came for Mahina. He was so fast.'

'Your friend murdered the lanista's guards,' Erik said. 'The lanista will not take kindly to that.'

'Dimitri did it to protect the lanista's daughter,' Almond said.

'He will need proof of that,' Hans said, adjusting Jarod.

'Who do you think did this, Erik?' Almond said. 'Who wants to hurt the lanista this badly?'

'Gron,' Hans said. 'His lanista has done this. I am certain of it.'

'Do you think he would be this bold, Hans?' Erik said.

'Maybe not Gron, but I feel the lanista of Ludus Leo is capable,' Hans said.

They walked through the noisy entertainment district. Revellers stared at the bleeding boy who hung off Hans's shoulder. At the north–south road, they turned south and walked until they reached the amphitheatre's western entrance. The guard who had let them out earlier that evening raised both his eyebrows as he held the door open.

'Get the medicus,' Hans said. 'Tell him to meet us in our cage.'

The guard bowed and ran off into the tunnels. Hans walked slowly, taking care not to hit Jarod's head against the walls. When they got to their room, Almond held open the door.

'What is going on here?' the magistrus said. 'What is that dog doing here?'

'Gron,' Hans said, lowering Jarod onto a cot. 'His lanista has taken Mahina.'

'What do you mean? A hit on the lanista's daughter?' The magistrus blinked rapidly. 'Surely someone isn't that stupid.'

'It is Gron's lanista,' Hans said, sneering. 'I am going to make that man pay for what he has done.'

'Are we sure this is the case?' the magistrus said, looking at Erik. 'It will bring dishonour to the lanista's entire ludus.'

Erik shrugged. 'It is the only thing we can think of.'

'We don't know for sure,' Almond said. 'I need to find Dimitri and see what he is up to.'

'Dimitri?' the magistrus said. 'Your friend? Why is he involved?'

'Dimitri killed two of the lanista's guards to save Mahina,' Almond said. 'Jarod here saw the whole thing.'

The magistrus turned red. He opened his mouth, but no words came out.

'It is true,' Jarod croaked. 'The knife slinger killed the guards. He said he was saving Mahina from the dogs that were on their way to kill her.'

'Do you know this for sure, Jarod?' the magistrus said, his voice a whisper. 'The lanista's guards are sacred to him.'

'It is what the knife slinger said,' Jarod said.

'Step aside,' the medicus said, marching through the room to get to Jarod. He took one look at him, then pointed at each guard. 'You get cloths. You get water. You hold up his head.'

Two guards ran out of the room. Another knelt and cradled Jarod's head.

The sound of tearing cloth filled the room. 'Someone has stabbed and sliced him,' the medicus said. 'He has lost a lot of blood.'

'Will he be OK, Medicus?' Almond said, kneeling.

'They didn't hit any organs or veins,' the medicus said. 'I think we caught him just in time. Another hour and we would be burying him.'

Almond stood. 'I need to find Dimitri, Hans.'

'We cannot leave now,' Hans said. 'Our number will be called this afternoon.'

'But I can help,' Almond said. 'Can we not postpone any fights?'

'No,' Erik said, lowering his voice. 'If you want to help, make sure you don't die in the arena.'

Almond watched Erik stalk out of the room.

The medicus stood and signalled to the guards. 'Take him and the dog back to the carriage. Make sure we have guards posted.'

The guards saluted, then gently picked up the cot Jarod lay on. Another picked up a growling Scrappy. Their footsteps, in unison, echoed off the corridor walls.

'It would be good for the both of you to rest,' the medicus said. 'You will both be fighting soon and it will be a tougher match than this morning's.'

Hans walked over to his coat, lay down, and started snoring before his head hit the pillow.

'You will wake me with any news?' Almond said to the magistrus.

The magistrus nodded a yes, but his eyes said no.

'It's time,' Hans said, slapping Almond's foot.

Almond sat up and rubbed his eyes. 'Time?'

'Time to fight,' Hans said.

'Unbelievable.' Almond looked up at the ceiling.

'We are fighting a gladiator who comes from Gron's ludus,' Hans said. 'They fight dirty.'

'This is a dirty business,' Almond said, slipping on his sandals. 'Have we any news about Mahina?'

'Your friend, the knife slinger, has contacted Erik,' Hans said. 'He will only deal with you.'

Almond stopped adjusting his clothes. 'Why didn't you wake me?'

'Because we need to fight,' Hans said, raising an eyebrow. 'And you needed your rest.'

'Are you being serious?' Almond said. 'I don't care about this fight. I need to speak to Dimitri and find out about Mahina.'

'You are not going anywhere except in this arena,' Hans said. 'Like Erik said, help by winning this fight first.'

Almond gritted his teeth. 'Stupid games. Stupid arena. Stupid screaming crowd. Stupid everything.'

Hans snorted as the corners of his mouth turned up. 'You done with your extravagant cursing?'

'Let's get this stupid round of fighting over and done with,' Almond said, stalking towards the cell door.

'OK, then,' Hans said, following Almond through the door.

'Come on,' Almond said.

'Are you two ready?' the lanista said.

Almond and Hans swung around.

The lanista stared straight at Almond with unblinking eyes.

'We are ready, sir,' Hans said, lifting himself to his tallest height. 'For Ludus Capri.'

'I know about my daughter, servant,' the lanista said. 'Win this fight so we can speak to your friend and I can get my daughter back.'

The muscles in Almond's jaw popped. 'We will see you in a moment, sir.'

The lanista nodded, turned, and marched towards the lift leading to the seating area.

'Let's get this done, Hans,' Almond said as the door swung open.

The roar of the crowd made Almond wince. He made his way to the earth quadrant where he turned and watched the other contestants enter the arena. Immediately, he identified the gladiator who belonged to Ludus Leo.

'What a peacock,' Hans said, looking at the same gladiator. 'He walks with arrogance and ego.'

'His servant is more deadly,' Almond said, his voice rising above the crowd. 'Beware of dirty tactics from him.'

Hans's eyes narrowed as he scanned the small man walking behind the gladiator. 'He looks dangerous.'

'A beaten man with nothing to live for,' Almond said. 'We need to get rid of him quickly.'

The man on the podium walked to the end of the rail. Almond followed Hans into the middle of the arena. After a brief introduction of the four ludi, the man signalled for the gladiators and servants to get back into their quadrants. A moment later, the loud blast of the oversized alphorn resonated through the amphitheatre.

The first panel slammed open. Hans pulled out a small, round shield and a small spear. Almond pulled out a long trident.

'Swap?' they both said together.

They swapped weapons and turned to see Ludus Leo already sending a gladiator and his servant to their deaths.

'That servant is filled with rage,' Hans said.

'Something is wrong here,' Almond said, looking at the other gladiator. 'Those two are up to something.'

Hans growled. 'They are working together and we are next.'

Almond looked up to the heavens while he held his medallion. 'I am sorry.'

'What are you doing?' Hans said, spreading his hands.

'Apologising to dead loved ones,' Almond said, shrugging. 'Just in case they choose to tell me off after I die.'

'Not today,' Hans said. 'Not today.'

The two gladiators and their servants charged Almond and Hans. Almond bent his knees, spun, and flung the small shield like a spinning top. The edge slammed into the gladiator's nose and sent him flying. His servant skidded to a stop before turning and running away. Hans engaged with the gladiator from Ludus Leo. Almond spun and drove his spear at the Ludus Leo servant, stopping his knife from entering Hans's kidney. The servant turned, screamed, and charged Almond. In a flash, Almond spun, ducked, and drove his spear straight through the servant. With wide eyes, the servant collapsed. The gladiator from Ludus Leo, distracted by the quick death of his servant, seemed to lose track of Hans's trident. A second later, he fell face-first into the dirt.

Almond turned to the remaining servant. 'Go. Tell your lanista we know what you did. We know you worked together.'

The servant hung his head. 'My lanista will kill me.'

'Tell him,' Almond shouted.

The servant looked back at the wooden door, then at Hans. He took a deep breath, shouted, and charged. A moment later, the light left his eyes and Hans pulled the trident from him.

'Well, that was a waste,' Almond said, walking back to the door. Just before the door, he stopped and looked back at Hans. The big gladiator worked the crowd with fist pumps and chest thumps.

'What?' Hans said, jogging over to Almond with a small grin on his face.

'Just move, will you?' Almond said, rolling his eyes.

'I am entertaining the crowd,' Hans said.

'I will recommend you join the circus rather than the Queen's Guard,' Almond said over his shoulder. 'Move it, Hans. We need to speak to Dimitri.'

The wooden door creaked open. Almond stalked through, then stopped in his tracks. At the end of the corridor, Gron and his lanista stood staring.

'What do you want, Gron?' Hans hollered. 'Did you think you could send one of your juniors to best us?'

'Come on, Hans,' Almond said, walking up to the gate to their quarters. 'We don't have time for this.'

'Your days are done, Hans,' Gron shouted.

Hans gave Gron a rude sign.

Gron returned the gesture.

Hans joined Almond in the large cell.

'The lanista is on his way,' Erik said, eyeing Almond.

‘Yes, Erik, I saw it too,’ Hans said, looking at Almond.

‘I have not seen someone move that fast in a long time,’ Erik said. ‘Not since the last time I saw a knife slinger fight.’

Almond ignored them both and sat cross-legged on the floor.

‘You’re a knife slinger, aren’t you?’ Erik said.

The metal door swung open. The lanista walked in, making all the gladiators and servants fall quiet.

Almond stood.

‘This Dimitri wishes to speak to you alone,’ the lanista said.

‘Bring him here, sir,’ Almond said, spreading his hands.

‘He has refused,’ the lanista said.

‘Then let us go to him,’ Almond said.

‘We cannot,’ the lanista said. ‘Ludus Leo is waiting to ambush you in the corridors. If you leave now, there will be all out war in the hypogeum.’

Erik cleared his throat. ‘Sir, I think it is time you leave and go to your carriage. Jarod needs you.’

The lanista looked at Erik with confusion. He opened his mouth, then closed it as he realised what was being asked. ‘I think that is a good idea, Erik. I hope you all get a good night’s sleep.’

‘We will, sir,’ Erik said.

The lanista disappeared out of the door and Erik waited until it banged shut.

‘You may visit Dimitri this evening,’ Erik said. ‘Be back before sunrise.’

‘Yes, sir,’ Almond said.

Erik turned and walked out of the room.

‘Get some sleep,’ Hans said. ‘And by the way, I am coming with you tonight.’

‘That is a bad idea,’ Almond said.

‘I don’t care what type of idea it is,’ Hans said, walking back to their blankets. ‘I will escort you tonight. Let us eat.’

Almond sat on his blanket and reached for the delicious plate of fruit and meats they had left for him.

'Winning games has its perks,' Hans said with a mouth full of food. 'The General is very generous.'

'If you come tonight, don't get into a fight with Dimitri,' Almond said.

'He must not start with me then,' Hans said.

Almond turned and stared straight at Hans. 'I am being serious. You are a formidable warrior, but Dimitri will kill you in seconds. Please don't get into a fight with him.'

Hans narrowed his eyes before taking a deep breath. 'If you say so, servant.'

With a sigh and a shake of his head, Almond lay down on his blanket and closed his eyes.

A hand snaked over Almond's mouth. His eyes shot open.

'Quiet,' Hans said. 'There is trouble.'

Almond nodded once.

'Gron and his ludus have been plotting and planning through the night,' Hans said. 'I am not sure we can make it out to see your friend.'

Almond placed his feet into his sandals. He closed his eyes and took in a deep, long breath. 'We have to try, Hans. Mahina and the lanista are counting on us.'

Hans looked over at the door to their cell. A guard stood with his shoulder up against the door frame. 'I think Erik has left that guard there to help us.'

'He can give Dimitri a signal for me,' Almond said.

'What would the signal be?' Hans said, raising his eyebrows.

Almond tapped two fingers on the inside of his wrist, then formed an X with his index fingers.

‘What does it mean?’ Hans said.

‘It means we are compromised and we cannot join him,’ Almond said. ‘We then have to wait to see what he wants to do.’

‘That is risky,’ Hans said. ‘We are relying on this knife slinger to do the right thing.’

‘Let us decide once the guard has given the signal,’ Almond said. ‘We will know pretty soon if Dimitri is serious.’

Hans walked over to the guard and whispered in his ear. The guard nodded. Hans showed the guard the sign. The guard marched down the corridor.

Hans came back and sat with Almond. ‘Definitely left by Erik to help us.’

‘Don’t get too comfortable,’ Almond said, smiling. ‘We might need to move quickly.’

‘I don’t understand?’ Hans said.

‘If Dimitri wants to speak to us, he will speak to us.’ Almond checked his sandals and clothes, then walked up to the gate. ‘We may have to move quickly if he asks us to.’

Hans joined him and leant against the gate. He picked at his fingernails. A few minutes later, a shout sounded down the corridor.

‘Quicker than I thought,’ Almond said, grinning at Hans. ‘Let’s go.’

Footsteps sounded through the corridors. More shouts echoed through the hypogeum. Halfway down one corridor, Almond slammed a rapid combination of punches into a man. The man doubled over, sound asleep.

‘Unbelievable,’ Hans whispered.

After a few turns, Almond slowed. At the end of the long corridor stood the amphitheatre’s exit. Steel slashed through the air quicker than the eye could see.

‘Dimitri,’ Almond said, over his shoulder. ‘Stick close to me.’

Hans grunted as he moved closer to Almond. Another shout

sounded near the amphitheatre exit. Almond stepped over a few lifeless bodies.

'One of Ludus Leo's,' Hans said. 'These were the ones waiting for us.'

As they neared the exit, Almond slowed and waited.

'Go now,' Dimitri said, twisting away from a knife before elbowing a servant in the face. 'Go to the blacksmiths district.'

Almond dodged a slashing sword, then ran up the ramp to the exit. The gate stood open. The guard from their cell directed them to the south.

'Thank you,' Hans said to the guard. 'Get back to our room and don't get killed on the way.'

Almond blasted a quick whistle down the ramp. Dimitri turned and Almond signalled to him to let the guard through.

'I saw at least four dead people,' Hans said. 'All men from Ludus Leo.'

'They were waiting for us, alright,' Almond said. 'We would be dead if we had tried to get through.'

'The lanista of Ludus Leo is going to get back at our lanista,' Hans said, with a worried backwards glance.

'This is a chance he will want us to take,' Almond said. 'His daughter is at stake.'

They made their way down the north–south road until they reached the road to the blacksmiths district.

'Where do we go from here?' Hans said.

Almond looked at the big man and shrugged. 'I guess we walk slowly down the road?'

They turned into the blacksmiths district and walked slowly past the big black buildings.

'The famous district,' Hans said, his eyes filled with wonder. 'The place where they make the world's best weapons.'

Almond smiled at Hans. 'You are right. They say the blacksmiths here are better than the blacksmiths in the City of Lynn.'

Up ahead, a shadowy figure stepped out onto the street.

Hans put a hand on Almond's shoulder to stop him.

Almond looked ahead and narrowed his eyes. 'Who are you?' he said, eventually.

The figure stood still.

'Gentlemen,' Dimitri said from behind them.

Hans spun and moved to a fighting stance.

'Relax please, Hans,' Almond said, reaching up and putting his hand on his shoulder.

'I am relaxed,' Hans said, straightening up and giving Dimitri the eye.

'Where is she?' Almond said. 'What have you done with Mahina?'

'She is right there,' Dimitri said, pointing past him.

Almond turned and saw Mahina standing next to the dark figure. He turned to Dimitri. 'What is the meaning of this?'

Dimitri walked past them and beckoned them to follow. 'It is OK, friend. Follow me.'

Hans placed a hand on Almond's shoulder. 'I don't like this.'

'Nor do I,' Almond said, stepping forward. 'But what choice do we have?'

The hooded figure raised his head the closer they got. Once Almond and Hans were within a speaking distance, the hooded figure lifted his hood and let it drop over his shoulders.

'General,' Hans said, his hand slamming onto his chest and his head bowing.

Almond frowned. 'What is going on, Mahina?'

Mahina stepped forward. 'I am OK, Almond. I promise.'

'What is going on?' Almond repeated. 'Dimitri? General?'

The General raised a hand. 'I need your help, gentlemen.'

'Anything,' Hans said, raising his chin.

'Hang on, Hans,' Almond said. 'The General of Battleacre

slinking through the shadows is highly unusual. I need convincing. Again, what is going on here?'

'It is my son,' the General said. 'They have my son.'

'Who has your son?' Almond said.

'The vampires,' the General said.

CHAPTER 5
A ROYAL?

Almond turned to Dimitri. 'You set this up.'

Dimitri smiled. 'I would never do such a thing.'

The General cleared his throat. 'I set it up and I am sorry we must meet this way. The world's lanistae mustn't know of my son's predicament.'

'Why have the vampires taken your son?' Almond said. 'They know the folly in doing something so stupid. It will start a war.'

The General looked at Hans. 'Ludus Leo. Your arch-rivals. They are making a grab for the city of Battleacre. If I submit, and my son is not here to take my place, they will choose a lanista to take the mantle.'

'How are they planning to take Battleacre?' Almond said.

The General rubbed his chin. 'They have threatened to kill my son if I do not submit.'

Hans growled. 'His dishonour knows no bounds. I will lift their lanista's head from his shoulders.'

'What does that have to do with the vampires?' Almond said. 'Why are they involved?'

'We don't know,' Mahina said. 'There is a rumour Ludus Leo's lanista is holding one of their royals. A young woman named Genevie.'

'Or the vampires want more control of Battleacre,' the General said. 'We don't know.'

Almond raised his eyebrows at Dimitri. 'And you? How are you involved in this?'

'You know Dimitri is a member of the knife slingers? He's in the Queen's Guard,' the General said. 'I have asked him to get my son back. He has agreed, but he said he cannot do this alone.'

'Mahina's capture was to draw me out,' Almond said. 'You killed two guards to draw me out, Dimitri?'

He snorted. 'I don't kill people indiscriminately, Almond. Vampires are hunting Mahina down. Your guards would have led her right to them. I needed to act quickly.'

'He saved my life,' Mahina said. 'I would be with the vampires right now.'

'Heads must roll,' Hans growled. 'The stain of Ludus Leo and its lanista needs to be wiped off this world. How dare they bring dishonour on the city of Battleacre!'

'We need to use our heads before our muscles, Hans,' Almond said. 'Vampires are a very dangerous foe.'

'Getting soft in your old age, brother?' Dimitri said, smiling.

'You could have warned me of all of this, Dimitri,' Almond said. 'We could have saved those guards' lives.'

The General took a step forward. 'We can dissect our decisions over ale when we have solved our problems. Right now, I would like to find my son. Can you help us?'

'We will need to be freed from our lanista and given the keys to the city, sir,' Hans said.

'Hang on, Hans,' Almond said, raising a finger. 'I don't think that is a good idea. We need to maintain our cover. Ludus Leo will be suspicious if we suddenly gain freedom to wander the city.'

Dimitri nodded. 'I think you are right. You two tackle Ludus Leo and try to find out about this royal. I will tackle the vampires.'

'That means you will need to continue fighting in the arena,' the General said.

Dimitri chuckled. 'I am sorry, General, but Almond here has been taking you on a little ride. The arena is not a problem for a knife slinger.'

'I knew it,' Hans said.

'Not any knife slinger,' Dimitri said. 'A master weapons-smith knife slinger.'

'That is enough, Dimitri,' Almond said. 'You know the code.'

Dimitri bowed his head.

'What is a weapons-smith knife slinger?' Hans asked.

Dimitri raised an eyebrow at Almond. 'You really have been holding back, haven't you?'

'I am a knife-slinger blacksmith,' Almond said. 'I was trained in the art by a master long-forgotten.'

Hans shook his head. 'I knew you were important, Almond, but this news I would never have guessed.'

Dimitri tutted. 'He is important enough for the knife slingers to be looking for him. Some debts are yet to be paid.'

'These are issues we do not need to be a part of,' the General said.

'What can I do?' Mahina said, seeing the discomfort growing in Almond's face.

'You are going back to the carriage,' Almond said. 'Your father will rip this town apart if he cannot find you.'

'But I would like to help,' Mahina said.

'Your job will be to keep the world looking normal, Mahina,' Almond said. 'Ludus Leo will be on their toes, seeing you returned to the carriage.'

'Ludus Leo and the vampires will both know there is a third party involved,' the General said.

'My father will ask what happened to me,' Mahina said.

'Tell him it was the vampires that captured you, but someone helped you escape,' Almond said.

'He will seek out the perpetrators,' Hans said. 'He will not dismiss something like this.'

'Leave that with me,' the General said. 'I can say we have dealt with the vampires.'

Almond rubbed his chin. 'Make sure Ludus Leo hears of this.'

'What of my son, though?' the General said. 'Will all of this not put his life at risk?'

'Your son will need to be kept alive until Ludus Leo takes over the city of Battleacre,' Almond said. 'If your son is not in the picture, they cannot blackmail you.'

The General ran a hand over his face. 'I am not thinking clearly. The capture of my son has clouded my judgement.'

'We need to trust what Almond says,' Dimitri said. 'This is why I have drawn him out. He has a knack for understanding mind games.'

Almond narrowed his eyes at Dimitri. 'And Dimitri here has a knack for dramatics.'

'We must get moving,' Hans said. 'Dimitri has left a trail of bodies. Questions will be asked. We need to get back into our cell.'

'Jarod is back at the carriage,' Almond said, looking at Mahina. 'Scrappy is with him.'

'I will take Mahina back to the carriage now,' the General said.

'I will start the search for the General's son,' Dimitri said. 'They cannot be hiding him too far away.'

'And we will get some information about this vampire who is being held,' Almond said.

Hans cleared his throat. 'We need to move.'

'Thank you,' the General said, pulling the hooded cloak over his head.

'I will be in touch, brother,' Dimitri said. 'Find out as much information as you can from Ludus Leo.'

'How do we intend to share information?' Almond said.

'Can you trust the guard that signalled me?' Dimitri said.

Hans nodded. 'He will do as I ask.'

'Stay safe, brother,' Almond said, looking at Dimitri. 'Vampires are a worthy foe.'

Dimitri tilted his head to one side and tapped the knives on his belt.

'It has been an honour, General,' Hans said, slamming his fist against his breast.

'Be safe, gladiator,' the General said, then disappeared into the shadows.

'Time to go, Hans.' Almond turned and walked back through the blacksmiths district.

They reached the north–south road, then jogged up to the amphitheatre's western gate. The guard stepped out of the shadows.

Hans leant in and whispered into his ear. The guard nodded, then walked down the long ramp.

'He is going to take us another way,' Hans said over his shoulder. 'It seems Ludus Leo has regrouped and is looking for us.'

The three men's footsteps echoed through the hypogeum as they followed the twisting and turning tunnels. The guard slowed as they reached their cell. A man with a sword pock-marked with the signs of many skirmishes stepped out of the shadows. Almond grabbed the guard by his collar and pulled him backwards just as the sword struck the ground. Hans jumped forward and slammed his fist against the man's nose. An almighty crack sounded through the corridors as the man collapsed in a heap.

'Let's get to the cell.' Almond hissed. 'Leave him.'

Hans sneered at the unconscious man as he stepped over him. They ran through the rest of the corridors until they got to Ludus

Capri's cage. The guard took in a deep breath and stilled his shaking hands. He opened the door and ushered Almond and Hans into the cell.

'Get some rest,' Hans said as they made their way through the sleeping gladiators. 'I have a feeling the next few matches in the arena will not be easy.'

Almond kicked off his sandals and lay on the bed with his hands interlaced under his head. 'How do you suggest we find out about this captured vampire?'

'I have no idea,' Hans muttered, then promptly fell asleep.

The roaring crowd deafened Almond. He took a deep breath and looked up at the heavens.

'You ready, servant?' Hans said, walking back into the quadrant. 'Ludus Leo has sent in their second-best gladiator.'

Almond looked across into the other quadrant at the mountain of a man. 'The servant is as big as you.'

'And a formidable warrior,' Hans said.

'How is it possible a gladiator can have another gladiator as a servant?' Almond said.

'He is a defeated gladiator Ludus Leo purchased as a servant,' Hans said. 'It is a way around the rules but frowned upon.'

The gamekeeper announced the different houses. After the sound of the oversized alphorn rang through the arena, the first panel slammed open. Hans pulled out two small hammers. Almond pulled out a pole twice his size.

'Swap?' they both said in unison.

With a chuckle, Almond caught the two small hammers, weighing them in his hands. He turned and watched two of the gladiators and their servants wage war in the middle of the arena. The Ludus Leo gladiator ignored the fighting and stared at Hans.

‘You know each other?’ Almond said. ‘He seems to be giving you the loving eyes of a predator about to catch his prey.’

Hans grunted. ‘We have history.’

‘Just great,’ Almond said.

The four fighters in the middle of the arena began to tire. A few moments later, the servant of the Ludus Leo gladiator weighed in and ended them all. The fifth panels slammed open.

Almond looked at the two hammers, then tossed them onto the ground.

Hans picked up his greatsword by its charcoal-black hilt and Almond retrieved his two short swords.

‘Um, Hans?’ Almond said, pointing to his weapon.

Hans flipped the sword onto its side, then cursed. Rust etched through the entire blade.

‘Mine too,’ Almond said, showing him the two short swords. ‘These won’t take one hit from any weapon.’

‘And we cannot take weapons from the other panels,’ Hans said. ‘We are stuck with these.’

With an almighty roar, the opposing gladiator ran towards them. The opposing servant ran next to his gladiator and, seeing Almond, he let out a long growl.

Almond flicked one short sword over, holding the blade’s point. He jumped high and with a flick of the wrist, he sent the blade twirling through the air. The servant flicked his weapon at the blade, deflecting it to the side. Before he could bring his weapon back to defend, Almond drove the other short sword through him. The servant stared at the sword that stuck through his chest, then swung his weapon at Almond. The short sword Almond used to defend himself snapped, sending the blade flying. Almond kicked out his foot and sent the servant crashing to the ground.

Hans dodge-rolled under the gladiator’s weapon. He swung his greatsword, then stared in disbelief as it shattered into pieces.

'You and your servant have no weapons, Hans,' the gladiator said. 'I would ask you to submit, but you know I will not accept.'

'Your house has brought shame on the games,' Hans said, spitting at the gladiator's feet. 'You fight with no honour.'

'What is honour if you are dead?' the gladiator said. 'It is nothing. Nothing.'

Almond walked sideways to circle the gladiator.

'I see you, servant,' the gladiator said, pointing his two-bladed axe at Almond.

'What is your lanista up to?' Hans said. 'We know he is trying to capture Battleacre.'

The gladiator sneered. 'Ludus Leo will rule these lands. Battleacre's people and the vampires.'

'Who has he captured?' Almond said. 'Which one of the vampires has he got?'

The crowd grew restless as the three men stalked each other.

'She is a beautiful woman,' the gladiator said, lunging at Hans. 'Chained and watched day and night.'

Hans rolled away from the axe.

'A royal?' Hans said.

'Enough talking,' the gladiator said. 'I will take both your heads and bring honour to Ludus Leo.'

'The vampire is definitely not a royal vampire,' Almond said, continuing to circle. 'The royal vampire is not good-looking.'

'She is very good-looking,' the gladiator said, swinging his axe.

'A royal vampire then,' Hans said, backtracking away from the swinging axe. 'What is her name, gladiator?'

The gladiator realised the trap he had just fallen into, and so he roared and charged at Hans. Almond dived forward and smacked the gladiator's ankle, sending him stumbling to the ground. Hans grabbed a handful of arena sand and threw it in the gladiator's face. The gladiator jumped to his feet and blindly swung his double-sided axe. Almond picked up the hilt of Hans's shattered greatsword. A small piece of blade protruded from the hilt.

'I am over here, gladiator,' Hans said, seeing Almond sneak up behind the giant man. The gladiator swung his axe in a wide arc. Almond dodged in and slashed the last piece of blade against the gladiator's ankles. With a scream, the man fell to his knees.

'What is her name?' Almond said into the giant man's ear. 'Tell me her name and we will let you live.'

'I will tell you nothing,' the gladiator spat. 'My lanista will hang me. I would rather die a warrior.'

'Where is she being kept?' Almond said. 'Tell me, warrior.'

The gladiator struggled to his feet, but his ankles wouldn't hold him. He fell again onto the ground.

'Where is she being held?' Almond said. 'I have searched Ludus Leo and have found nothing. Where are they keeping her?'

The gladiator looked at Almond with confusion.

'So, she is being held near Ludus Leo,' Almond said. 'Where is she? On the lower levels?'

'You will never find her,' the gladiator said. 'And even if you did, you wouldn't get anywhere near her.'

The crowd began to boo.

'Get up,' Hans said.

'Leave him, Hans,' Almond said. 'The shame of not ending with a warrior's death is the best thing for him.'

'No,' the gladiator said. 'It is code, Hans. Do not let it end this way.'

Hans bent down and picked up the two-sided axe. 'Tell me who it is. Where is she being held?'

The gladiator hung his head. 'Her name is Genevie. She is in the lower areas of the hypogeum. Underneath Ludus Leo. You will never get near her.'

In one swift move, Hans swung the axe and lifted the gladiator's head from his shoulders.

The crowd roared its approval. Hans marched around the arena with his hands in the air. The crowd cheered louder. Then suddenly, silence. Almond looked up at the podium. The General stood with his hands behind his back, waiting.

Almond walked over to where Hans stood. 'What is he doing?'

'I do not know,' Hans said.

'Citizens of Battleacre,' the General said, raising his hands. 'I call on all lanistae to join us in the arena.'

'Don't do anything silly,' Almond said under his breath.

The wooden doors opened and two guards trotted out and stood next to Hans and Almond. One by one, a lanista from each ludus walked into the arena.

'My friends,' the General said, placing his hands on the railing and looking down at the lanistae. 'The Queen of the City of Lynn has increased the rewards for winning these exceptional games.'

The crowd murmured, then hushed.

'Whichever ludus wins these games will challenge me for the leadership of Battleacre,' the General said. 'I will enter my house into the tournament.'

The lanistae looked at each other with raised eyebrows.

'What are you up to, General?' Almond whispered.

'Lanistae, here are my champions who shall enter the fight,' the General said.

Dimitri and another thin man wearing a long cloak appeared next to the General.

Almond sucked air between his teeth. 'What is Dimitri doing there?'

'It is customary for each house to choose a champion,' the General said. 'Here is my champion. Dimitri, who once fought in the very arena you now stand in, and his servant, Damsk.'

'Both knife slingers,' Almond whispered. 'This will not be a fair fight.'

Hans nudged Almond and placed a finger on his lips.

'Select your champions, lanistae,' the General said. 'Over the next three days, our champions will fight to the last man standing. The games will begin tomorrow morning.'

The crowd stamped their feet. 'Fight, fight, fight.'

'Whoever wins these games will challenge my team to see who wins the leadership of Battleacre,' the General said.

The lanistae turned and made for the wooden doors. When they were all through, the guards let Almond and Hans through the doors and into their large cell. Ludus Capri stood silent as their lanista waited for Almond and Hans to enter.

'What do you know of this?' the lanista said, stepping in front of Hans. 'What is going on?'

Hans glanced at Almond.

The lanista poked Hans in the chest. 'You belong to me,' he thundered. 'You do not need this servant's approval to speak.'

Hans cleared his throat. 'The General's son has gone missing. He thinks the vampires have taken him under the request of Ludus Leo. It seems Ludus Leo is holding one of the royal vampires, thus blackmailing the vampires to hold the General's son.'

The lanista took a step backwards.

'He has entered his champions to prevent this,' Almond said. 'Or to at least slow things down.'

'A brave move, knowing his son is being held captive,' the lanista said. 'I would tear this place apart.'

Almond sighed. 'He is doing his duty. Battleacre is more important than his son.'

The lanista grunted. 'It will kill him to lose his son. He would not survive such a tragedy.'

'His son is dating your daughter,' Hans said.

Almond kicked Hans hard in the shin. Hans sucked in a breath.

'No need to kick your gladiator, servant,' the lanista said, smiling. 'I know exactly what is going on with my daughter and I will thank the General's champion for saving her.'

‘I didn’t expect you not to know,’ Almond said. ‘I just need a good excuse to kick Hans.’

Almond saw the muscle in Hans’s cheek twitch as he tried hard not to smile.

The lanista turned to a guard. ‘Go and find Erik for me, please. We need to discuss the best form of action.’

The guard bowed once and hurried out of the cell. The lanista inclined his head at the area where Hans and Almond slept. Another guard ran forward with a small wooden bench. The lanista took a seat. Almond and Hans sat on their blankets and looked up at him.

‘Tell me about the General’s champion,’ the lanista said.

‘He is a knife slinger,’ Hans said, glancing at Almond. ‘According to his own assessment, he is the second-best fighter in the city.’

‘And the first?’ the lanista said.

Hans looked at Almond.

‘I am not,’ Almond said. ‘Well, not anymore.’

‘A weapons master knife slinger,’ Hans said. ‘Dimitri seems somewhat in awe or afraid of our Almond here.’

Almond again kicked Hans in the shin.

The cage door slammed closed. The tall figure of Erik walked over to where they sat.

‘He knows,’ Almond said, looking at Erik, ‘about his daughter.’

Erik turned pale.

‘It is OK, my friend,’ the lanista said, indicating he should sit. ‘I am assuming she is safe?’

‘Very, sir,’ Erik said, sitting down. ‘I have guards posted in multiple positions and it seems Scrappy has turned into her guard dog.’

‘I think you have lost your best friend there,’ Hans said, leaning over and punching Almond on the shoulder.

The lanista rubbed his chin. He turned to Erik. 'Ludus Leo is blackmailing the vampires into detaining the General's son by holding a member of their royal family. We need to find where she is being held and we need to rescue her.'

Erik thought for a moment. 'If we free the royal vampire, then there will be no reason for them to hold the General's son.'

'My point exactly. Where do you think they have this royal?' the lanista said.

Hans cleared his throat.

'Please speak.'

'Their gladiator told us she is somewhere in the hypogeum underneath Ludus Leo,' Hans said.

'The gladiator spoke?'

'He did,' Almond said. 'He mentioned the vampire's name is Genevie.'

They nodded their heads.

'The champion games will distract everyone,' Almond said. 'That's when you could do a search.'

Erik stood. 'I will build a team to look for her. I will report back when I have information.'

'We would like to be part of that team,' Almond said.

'You have to fight,' the lanista said. 'I trust you are ready for the games. You will be fighting the best of the best.'

Hans stood and slammed his fist against his chest. 'We are ready, sir.'

With a nod of his head, the lanista turned and left the cell.

Hans dropped onto his blanket and let out a long sigh.

'Are you thinking what I am thinking?' Almond said.

'Your friend Dimitri and his servant?' Hans said. 'We will have to fight them.'

'We won't win,' Almond said. 'They are far superior to all of us.'

Hans kicked off his shoes and lay down. Almond did the same and interlaced his fingers behind his head.

'If we rescue this royal, we might not have to fight,' Almond said.

'That is out of our hands.'

'We need to help Erik,' Almond said. 'You heard what that gladiator said. They have her heavily guarded.'

Hans grunted.

'What do we do for the rest of the day?' Almond said.

'We rest,' Hans said. 'We will need all our strength for the games tomorrow. They will wake us up for food.'

Almond stared at the ceiling.

'You fought well today,' Hans said.

'Is that a compliment?'

'Don't push it, servant,' Hans said with a small chuckle.

Almond dozed off as the amphitheatre descended into silence.

'Psst.'

Almond's eyes popped open.

'Psst. Over here.'

He sat up and looked across the cell. Dimitri waved. Almond got up and walked over to the bars. 'What are you doing here? You are supposed to be hunting down the vampires.'

'All is not what it seems,' Dimitri said. 'Things we have been talking about have reached the ears of others.'

'What do you mean,' Almond said.

'Just watch your back,' Dimitri said, then disappeared up the corridor.

Almond stared after Dimitri.

‘What are you doing up?’ the magistrus said.

Almond spun around. ‘I thought I heard something. Do you know how the search is going?’

‘Erik has our people looking,’ the magistrus said. ‘I suggest you get back to bed and rest.’

Almond nodded, then wove his way back to his blanket. He lay down and stared at the ceiling.

CHAPTER 6

THE GENERAL'S CHAMPION

The crowd's feet stamped in unison.

'It has begun,' Hans said from the window. 'A game of champions.'

Almond pulled on his sandals, then made his way over to the window. Four lanistae stood in the centre of the arena. The announcer read out their names and which ludus they hailed from. As they announced each ludus, the lanista stepped forward and introduced their gladiators and servants.

'That will be us later today,' Hans said, his chest filling with pride. 'We will do our lanista proud, servant. What do you say?'

'I say we will get slaughtered by Dimitri and his friend is what I say,' Almond said.

'You have mentioned this already, servant,' Hans said. 'Let us die with honour then.'

'Or let us rescue this vampire so we don't have to fight them,' Almond said. 'How is Erik getting on with the search?'

'He has just finished speaking to the lanista,' Hans said, pointing over his shoulder with his thumb. 'He will tell us when he has news.'

Almond glanced over his shoulder at Erik.

'The lanistae are on their way out of the arena,' Hans said, his voice low.

Almond scanned the crowd and watched the betting men and women throw their coins at the bookmakers. He shook his head at the bloodlust in their eyes. The oversized alphorn rang through the afternoon skies. The champions fought with such force and determination that the arena walls rattled when one of them slammed into it. The servants slashed at each other, as vicious as their masters.

'The fights will last a lot longer,' Erik said, standing next to Hans and peering through the window. 'Are you up for this challenge?'

Hans growled at the window. His eyes narrowed and the veins in his neck popped. 'I want to bring honour to our ludus, sir.'

'That is good to hear,' Erik said. 'We got wind of where they are keeping the royal.'

Almond tore his eyes off the fight. 'Where?'

'One of our spies made it to Ludus Leo's animal enclosures, which were heavily guarded,' Erik said. 'They wouldn't normally guard that area so well.'

'We need to get into it to check,' Almond said.

'We have passed the information to the General,' Erik said. 'There is nothing we can do now. We need to wait to see what he does.'

Almond turned his head back to the fighting. The crowd stamped their feet even harder at the bloody spectacle on the arena floor. Finally, the second gladiator fell to the ground. The remaining champions ran to their quadrants and retrieved their favoured weapons.

'We need to watch,' Hans said. 'We may face them soon.'

Almond ignored Hans and returned to his blankets. He placed his hands over his ears to block out the sounds of the arena. 'All is not what it seems,' rang Dimitri's voice through his head. Almond scanned the cell and stopped as his eyes settled on the magistrus. Screams and shouts filled the arena. The magistrus stared at the backs of Erik and Hans. His eyes were full of hatred.

'All is not what it seems,' Dimitri's voice said.

'It is done. Are you OK?' Hans said, dropping onto his blanket.

Almond watched Erik walk over to the magistrus.

'I am OK,' Almond said. 'What do you think of Erik handing over the location to the General?'

'The General will act on it,' Hans said. 'He is in charge of Battleacre, so he has access to all of its areas.'

'I hope you are right,' Almond said, his eyes trained on Erik and the magistrus.

'Look who is here,' Hans said.

Almond climbed to his feet. 'How is he up and about?'

'Let's ask him, shall we?' Hans said, striding over to the cell bars.

Almond followed Hans to the end of the cell and waved over to Jarod. Mahina finished speaking to a guard, then walked over to the cell. In her arms, wrapped in a blanket, lay Scrappy.

'He is not allowed in here,' Jarod whispered. 'So we are hiding him.'

Almond smiled. 'He has never looked so comfortable. How are you doing, Jarod?'

'He should be in the carriage resting,' Mahina said, a look of concern in her eyes. 'His whole body is a stitch or a bandage.'

Jarod grinned. 'I am doing fine, sir. Just a little sore.'

'You should be resting,' Almond said. 'Mahina is right.'

'I wanted to come and see you to thank you both,' Jarod said, looking at Hans, then back at Almond. 'I wouldn't be alive if you hadn't found me.'

'You can thank that little dog,' Hans said. 'He brought us close to you.'

The alphorn sounded again. Everyone turned and waited for

the telltale noise of the first panel opening. A few moments later, the clash of steel on steel rang through the arena.

'Are you two ready for what's out there?' Mahina said.

'We have a weapons master knife slinger on our side,' Hans said, punching Almond on the shoulder. 'I am sure we will be OK.'

Jarod's eyes widened.

'I wish you wouldn't say that out loud,' Almond grumbled.

'What are your preferred weapons?' Jarod said.

Almond opened his mouth, then stopped to think. He looked at Mahina. 'My lady, can I ask you for a favour?'

'It depends what it is,' Mahina said.

'In the last match, our preferred weapons were rusted,' Almond said. 'Can you check this is not the case for the next fight?'

Mahina looked at Almond in confusion. 'You have told the magistrus of this?'

'We have,' Almond said. 'I would just like you to check for me that they have fixed it.'

'There is no need to worry the lanista's daughter with such a request,' Hans said, anger in his voice.

'It is OK, Hans,' Mahina said. 'I would happily help Ludus Capri's champion and his servant.'

Hans's chest swelled with apparent pride. Mahina gave Almond a small smile and a nod of her head.

'Back to your area,' the magistrus said, walking over. 'You both need your rest.'

'Thanks again,' Jarod said. 'We will be watching you fight.'

Almond and Hans walked back to their blankets.

'Why are you asking the lanista's daughter to check our weapons?' Hans hissed.

'Everything is not as it seems, Hans,' Almond said. 'Let us see what happens.'

Almond and Hans watched Mahina speak to the magistrus. She

smiled at the answers he gave her. When finished, she and Jarod both waved, before walking towards the lifts.

The wooden doors opened and in came a runner with a note. The magistrus read the note, then walked over to Almond and Hans. 'It is time,' he said. 'I do not have time to check your weapons, as per Mahina's request.'

'Who places our weapons in the panels?' Almond said.

'We hand the weapons to the gamekeeper personally,' the magistrus said. 'I can assure you I check them myself.'

'We must go,' Hans said, walking to the cell door.

'Are you both ready?' the lanista said, joining them on the ramp to the wooden doors.

'For Ludus Capri,' Hans said. 'We are always ready, sir.'

The three of them walked out into the blinding sunshine. As they walked to the middle of the arena, Almond checked their competition. No Ludus Leo. At the centre of the arena, they listened to the gamekeeper announce the ludus they came from. Once finished, the lanista made his way back through the wooden doors and Almond and Hans made their way to the earth quadrant.

'Ludus Scorpi, Ludus Libras and Ludus Arie,' Hans said. 'One from each element and all formidable.'

The alphorn sounded and the first panels slammed open. Hans pulled out a dagger and Almond pulled out a ball and chain.

'Yes, yes,' Hans said, handing the knife to Almond. 'Swap, right.'

Almond took the dagger and weighed it in his hands. Hans swung the ball around in a circle. Together, they jogged to the centre of the arena. Ludus Scorpi of the water element engaged first. Almond dodged and darted around Hans as he protected him from sneak attacks by the Scorpi servant. Suddenly, the Libra and Arie ludi both joined in.

'Back-to-back,' Almond shouted. 'Defence.'

Hans disengaged from the gladiator and stood back-to-back

with him. Slowly, the years of training returned to Almond. The fighting seemed to occur in slow motion. He darted in and out, jabbing and slicing at anyone who came close to his gladiator champion. After minutes of furious fighting, the first gladiator fell to his knees, then face-forward into the dirt. His servant followed shortly after. The three remaining gladiators continued to spar with their surprise weapons. As each was disarmed, they would sprint back to their quadrant and retrieve another weapon.

Hans took a blow to the side of his head. He dropped to one knee. The other two gladiators, sensing weakness, rounded on the fallen Hans.

Almond stalked around, while Hans slashed and hacked his two-sided axe at anyone who came close. A brave servant darted in but crashed face-first into the dirt. A gladiator jumped high into the air with his greatsword raised above his head. Before his feet could touch the ground, he landed, prone, in the dirt. The other gladiator and servant backed off, then ran to their quadrant to claim their preferred weapons.

'Can you get up?' Almond said, his eyes trained on the gladiator heading for his next weapon.

Hans shook his head, then pulled himself to his feet. 'My eyes cannot focus.'

'They will come back to you,' Almond said. 'We need to get our weapons.'

Hans held out a hand. 'Take me there.'

Almond pulled Hans along, and they ran back to their quadrant. He guided his hand into the fifth panel slot and waited until Hans pulled out his greatsword. Almond retrieved his two short swords, then growled in disgust.

'Rusted?' Hans asked. 'Please don't tell me they are broken.'

'As I expected,' Almond said. 'These weapons are not worthy. Someone in Ludus Capri is plotting our demise.'

Hans growled. 'I cannot believe someone would do that to our lanista.'

'Time to fight,' Almond said. 'Can you see yet?'

'Partially,' Hans said, walking towards the centre.

'You have been a warrior for decades,' Almond said. 'Trust your instincts. Trust what you can hear.'

They reached the centre of the arena where Ludus Aries waited. Hans spread his feet and tilted his head to one side.

'This is going to be too easy,' the Aries servant said. 'He cannot see.'

The Ludus Aries gladiator eyed Almond. 'It is not him we should be worried about.'

The servant circled.

'Servant behind us,' Almond said.

The Ludus Aries gladiator dived in. Almond parried the attacks from the long spear. Hans swung his greatsword in a wide arc, narrowly missing Almond but keeping the servant at bay. Almond darted forward and swung a short sword. The gladiator brought up his shield and smirked as the short sword shattered against it.

'It seems your ludus supplies inferior weapons,' the gladiator said.

Hans shouted out in pain. Almond swung around to see the servant darting in with a dagger. Almond's short sword sailed through the air and pierced the servant through the chest. A second later, he felt the tip of the gladiator's spear cut a gash in his side. Almond rolled away and came up into a crouch.

'What is happening?' Hans shouted. 'Are you OK, servant?'

The gladiator, seeing Almond without a weapon, turned on Hans. His spear attack was parried with Hans's swinging greatsword, but the large shield the gladiator held slammed into him, sending him onto his back.

The gladiator raised his spear and drove it forward. Almond

darted in and slammed himself against the gladiator's side. Slightly off balance, the spear drove into the dirt next to Hans.

The gladiator looked down in surprise as Hans drove his spear through the gladiator's chest.

'Roll, Hans,' Almond shouted.

Just before the gladiator hit the dirt, Hans rolled out of the way.

Slowly, the sound of the roaring crowd broke through the pounding of blood through Almond's ears.

Hans sat up and rubbed his eyes with the heels of his blood-soaked hands. Almond grabbed his shirt and lifted it to see a small cut down his side.

'Are you OK?' Hans said.

'Oh, now you can see,' Almond said, raising his eyebrows. 'That's just great.'

'He hit me pretty hard,' Hans said, struggling to his feet. 'Let's get back to the cell.'

'What, no working the crowd this time?' Almond said.

Hans grabbed Almond and threw him onto his shoulders. He walked a full circle of the arena as the crowd shouted, cheered and sang.

'Put me down, you idiot,' Almond said.

Hans dropped Almond onto his feet just before they reached the door to the hypogeum. The door swung open. The lanista stood there, smiling.

'Let's get you both in,' the medicus said. 'We can cheer your success in a bit.'

The lanista stepped out of the way. Almond and Hans made their way into the cell. The medicus lifted Almond's shirt and grunted. 'Superficial, but will get infected if we don't clean it.'

'I will do it,' Almond said. 'Hans needs attention first.'

The medicus moved away and began working on Hans.

Almond grabbed disinfectant and bandages from the medicus's bag and cleaned his wound.

'Well done, the both of you,' Erik said, walking up to them with a smile on his face. 'That was a well-fought match.'

Almond lay back on his blanket. 'Any news about the royal vampire?'

'I said it is with the General,' Erik said. 'We will wait for him.'

'I don't fancy fighting his champion and servant,' Almond said. 'He needs to act quickly.'

'We will fight with honour,' Hans said, his eyes a little crossed.

'He needs rest,' the medicus said. 'Lie on your blanket, but stay awake.'

'Yes, sir.'

'I will keep him awake,' Almond said.

The medicus and Erik left the cell to speak to the lanista.

'They are not searching for her,' Almond said. 'Hans, they have not told the General.'

Hans looked at Almond with clear eyes. 'I know. I knew there was something wrong when we retrieved those broken weapons.'

'You are a good actor, Hans,' Almond said with a smile. 'Tonight, I will look for her.'

'I am coming with you,' Hans said. 'My head is fine.'

Almond rested his head on the blanket and closed his eyes.

The amphitheatre descended into silence. Almond stared up at the ceiling. The crowds in the hypogeum dispersed, likely making their way to the entertainment district. Almond watched the lanista leave with the medicus and Erik. The magistrus lingered, making sure everything was taken care of. Eventually he, too, left.

'I am awake, servant,' Hans said from his blanket.

'Sure your big head is OK?' Almond said. 'It was an almighty blow.'

Hans chuckled. 'I still see blue dots occasionally. We need to find this royal.'

'Why the sudden urgency?' Almond said.

Hans sat up. 'There is a traitor within our organisation. That person is working for Ludus Leo.'

Almond finished putting on his sandals and rose from the blankets. 'Who do you think it is?'

'I do not wish to speculate,' Hans said. 'I have known this ludus for a very long time and I find it hard to imagine a traitor within its ranks.'

'I understand,' Almond said, making for the gate.

'Besides, I have also seen how you knife slingers fight. I think we have no chance with this Dimitri,' Hans said.

'I am glad you have come to your senses,' Almond said, signalling to the guard. 'We would have no chance against them, even with our preferred weapons.'

The guard unlocked the gate and handed a dagger to both Almond and Hans. Almond wound his way through the hypogeum towards Ludus Leo. After a few turnings, Almond halted at a corner.

'We need to get a few levels down,' Hans said. 'Up ahead is the Ludus Leo cell.'

Almond walked up the corridor and stopped at a ramp down to the next level. Next to the ramp, the lift trundled up from a different level.

'Too dangerous,' Almond said. 'We go down the ramp.'

They walked quietly down the ramp until they reached the next level. The noises of the General's servants echoed through the corridors. Almond turned back.

'Halt,' a man shouted.

Almond and Hans spun to see four Ludus Leo guards charge

them. The fight, brutal and quick, left all four guards dead in the corridor. Almond and Hans picked up swords from the guards' bodies.

'Nowhere to hide them,' Hans said. 'We will need to move quickly.'

They continued through the corridors until up ahead the kitchen and household servants' quarters of Ludus Leo appeared.

'Another level down,' Hans said, pointing to the next ramp.

Almond moved down the ramp, then stopped.

'What is it?' Hans said.

'Guards.' Almond tilted his head to one side. 'And a lot of them.'

'We can take them,' Hans said.

'What if there are gladiators down here?' Almond said. 'They would outmatch us with gladiators and guards.'

Hans shrugged. 'We have no choice, servant.'

'Let us get on with it then,' Almond said.

They sneaked down the ramp. Almond counted six guards lining the corridor leading towards the animal pens of Ludus Leo. He stood and walked down the corridor.

'Halt,' a guard shouted.

Shouts and screams echoed through the corridor as Almond and Hans dispatched the guards. More guards filtered up from the corridors. Slowly, Almond and Hans worked their way to the animal pens. At the entrance to the pens, a gladiator stood with his favoured weapon.

'Go into the pens and find the royal,' Hans said. 'I will take care of this.'

Almond darted into the pens. Hans's battle-cry echoed through the corridors. Almond walked up to the first pen and darted back as a striped cat jumped for the gate. At the next pen, a pig with almighty tusks snarled back at him. At the third, Almond stared into an empty stall filled with straw.

'This is it,' Almond thought.

He pushed the straw to one side. A trapdoor appeared. With a tug, it opened, revealing a set of wooden stairs. Almond walked down the stairs with his sword at the ready. At the bottom, a tunnel led downwards. With his sword poised, Almond waited for his eyes to adjust before he walked down the tunnel. The tunnel opened into a small chamber. Almond pressed himself to the corridor's wall as he approached the chamber.

'I can see you hiding there,' a woman's voice said.

Almond quickly looked into the chamber.

'Not like I can hurt you,' the woman's voice said.

Almond walked in. He stood and stared.

'Hello, Almond,' Genevie said.

'How do you know my name?'

'Master weapons-smith of the knife slingers order,' Genevie said with a smile that turned into a grimace. 'I have been alive for centuries. Your tales stretch far and wide.'

'I am no longer of that kind,' Almond said.

'You ran away without paying your debts, knife slinger,' Genevie said.

Almond instinctively grabbed and rubbed the medallion hanging from his neck.

Genevie smiled but with a look of sorry. 'The promise you made with your wife is the promise that killed her.'

The breath escaped Almond's lungs. His head dropped.

'You could have saved her, Almond,' Genevie said.

'She wouldn't have wanted me to hurt anyone,' Almond said. 'They were just kids playing the fool.'

Genevie let out a long, ragged breath.

Almond took a step forward. 'Genevie. Your kin are holding the General's son. They are doing it because they have you captured.'

Genevie's eyes turned a sliver. A growl escaped her lips. 'This will spark war between us. Vampires and humans.'

'I have come to free you so you can free the General's son.'

'I am not sure you can free me, Almond,' Genevie said.

Almond walked over to Genevie and knelt. A thin silver chain bit into her ankles. He stood and looked closely at Genevie's outstretched arms. Another silver chain cut deep into her skin with the ends secured onto a thick hook on the wall. Thick spikes were driven through each of Genevie's shoulders, and into the wall.

'I told you,' Genevie said. 'Even a weapons master of your skill cannot get this stuff off me.'

Almond smiled. 'I wouldn't be so quick to judge, Genevie.'

Almond pulled the medallion from his neck and removed it from his chain. He pressed its centre. The medallion popped open and out fell a tiny, shiny sliver of metal. Almond picked up the metal, spun it with the sharp end away, and inserted the blunt end back into the medallion.

'This blade is encrusted with a thin layer of diamond,' Almond said. 'It will cut through anything.'

Genevie chuckled. 'Only a master would have such a blade.'

Almond knelt and slipped the blade between Genevie's skin and the silver chain. He pulled towards himself and the chain popped. Genevie sucked in a long breath. Almond moved to the right wrist and cut the chain away. Then the left. The chain popped. Genevie still clung to the wall.

'I don't know how I can help you with those spikes,' Almond said.

'Stand back, master weapons-smith,' Genevie said.

Almond took a step back.

Genevie's fangs elongated. She growled, a deep rumbling primal sound. She placed her hands and feet on the wall and pushed. The spikes drove deeper into her shoulders. She pushed again and again. With a roar, she pushed the last part and fell to the ground. The two blood-soaked spikes stayed stuck in the walls.

Genevie rose. The wounds in her wrists, ankles and shoulders slowly closed. 'We need to go, Almond,' she said.

Almond packed away his miniature knife and made for the stairs. He helped Genevie climb to the top. The animals in the pens all went quiet as Genevie passed.

'How long till you get your strength back?' Almond said.

'I need to feed,' Genevie said.

'I would offer, but I don't feel like being dinner tonight.'

Genevie chuckled. 'I am sure we can find some of your enemies on the way.'

They made for the door.

'Hans,' Almond shouted, letting go of Genevie and running to the door. 'No, Hans.'

Hans's eyes lay open and lifeless. A sword stuck out of his chest. Next to him, the gladiator he fought lay face-down and lifeless.

'I never should have left him,' Almond said. 'He wasn't ready to fight.'

'You are right,' a voice said from the shadows. 'It was unwise to leave him.'

Genevie hissed.

Erik stepped out of the shadows. He held a long silver sword in his right hand and a thick silver dagger in his left.

'It was you,' Almond said. 'You changed our weapons.'

Erik ignored Almond and kept his eyes trained on Genevie. 'I see you have escaped my bonds, vampire. I will just end you here, now.'

Genevie backed away, her silver eyes trained on the sword and dagger.

Almond flew at Erik. On the way, he picked up a short sword. Erik took a step back in surprise as he blocked Almond's slashes.

'Catch,' Genevie shouted.

Almond caught the second short sword in his hand and dropped into his familiar knife-slinger stance.

Erik pulled his full focus onto Almond. The two of them danced into the corridor, slashing and parrying each other's weapons. Erik's silver sword nicked Almond's neck as he dodge-rolled out of the way.

Suddenly, Erik let out a scream. Genevie slammed her big vampire teeth into Erik's neck. He fell to his knees. Almond knocked the silver sword and dagger from his grasp. Genevie drank deeply until Erik fell into the dirt.

Almond turned and made his way back to Hans.

Genevie knelt next to Almond. 'Who is this?'

Almond looked at Genevie with tears in his eyes. 'He was the gladiator I fought with. He was my friend.'

Genevie placed a hand on his chest. 'He is not long dead.'

Almond looked at Genevie, opened his mouth, but hesitated.

'I can bring him back from the dead, if that is what you are asking?' Genevie said. 'But he will be one of my kin.'

Almond looked down at Hans. Then back at Genevie. 'I don't know what to do.'

A noise sounded from the corridor. Genevie flashed away. Screams echoed through the halls. Genevie returned with blood smeared across her lips and chin. All her wounds were practically healed.

'Can you take him back to Ludus Capri?' Almond said.

'You don't want me to bring him back?' Genevie said.

Almond dropped his head onto Hans's chest. The tears flowed. He lifted his head and looked at Genevie. 'He wanted to die in the arena. An honourable death.'

Genevie smiled. 'He has helped to save the General's son.'

Almond nodded. 'That is truly honourable. He had the greatest respect for the General.'

'Then let us take him to his ludus so this story can be told,' Genevie said, lifting Hans effortlessly. 'You will have to protect us, master knife slinger.'

Almond searched the area until he found the two short swords he had fought Erik with.

'You don't want the silver weapons?' Genevie said.

'They are only good for vampire hunting,' Almond said.

Genevie growled at the two weapons lying next to Erik.

He moved up the corridor until they reached the first ramp. At the top, guards charged at them. All of them landed in the dirt as Almond expertly used his short swords. At the next ramp, more guards came to their end. They climbed the second ramp. The guards, seeing Almond and Genevie, turned and fled.

'Word has got out,' Genevie said.

'They are petrified of you,' Almond said, over his shoulder.

'I was talking about you, knife slinger,' Genevie said.

Almond grunted and continued down the corridors. As they got closer to Ludus Capri, the crowds lining the corridor walls thickened. They reached the cage and Almond banged on the door. The lanista and the magistrus looked over with their mouths open.

'Open the gate,' Almond said.

The guard did as he was told. Genevie walked in and gently lay Hans on the ground. She turned to the lanista and said, 'Tell the General it was your gladiator that helped rescue his son.'

Before the lanista could open his mouth, Genevie was gone in a flash.

CHAPTER 7

THIS IS UNFAIR

The medicus knelt and checked Hans over. He looked up to the lanista and shook his head.

'What is the meaning of this, servant?' the lanista thundered.

'Erik,' Almond said, looking at Hans with his voice catching in his throat. 'Erik captured the royal vampire for Ludus Leo. It was him all along.'

'You are lying,' the lanista said, walking up to Almond. 'I have known Erik for over a decade. He would do nothing like this.'

'It is true,' Almond said. 'Genevie, the royal vampire, will confirm it.'

'And why should I believe some royal vampire?' the lanista said.

'You would do well to believe my brother, though,' Dimitri said, stepping out of the shadows. 'I have been down to the Ludus Leo animal pens, and I indeed saw your dead Erik down there.'

'He had formed a search party to look for her,' the lanista said.

'And he told you he had found the area and informed the General?' Dimitri asked. 'I can tell you he did not inform the General.'

The lanista stared at Dimitri.

He reached in to his cloak and pulled out the silver dagger. 'This is a vampire killer. It was owned by your number two lanista of Ludus Capri.'

The magistrus reached out and took the dagger. He turned it over in his hands.

'You have seen this before, haven't you?' Almond said, looking at the magistrus.

He let out a sigh. 'This is Erik's, sir. I have seen it before.'

The lanista placed his head in his hands. 'My ludus has brought dishonour to the General and to Battleacre.'

'It is not your fault,' Almond said.

'I am held accountable for all the actions of Ludus Capri,' the lanista said. 'The blame lies on my shoulders.'

'Lanista of Ludus Capri,' the General said, walking down the corridor. 'If I may have a word with you?'

The lanista took a step forward but stopped.

The magistrus held a hand across his body. 'The lanista will not leave our sight in this trying time. I ask that you address him in the safety of Ludus Capri.'

The General walked up to the lanista. 'You have helped rescue my son. For that, I am truly grateful. But it seems your house had a hand in his capture?'

The lanista pulled himself to his full height. 'Yes, General. It was one of mine who helped capture and hold the royal vampire.'

'Did you know of this man's intentions?' the General said, his eyes boring into the lanista's.

'My entire ludus and I were not aware of this,' the lanista said. 'But the responsibility falls on me. I will pull Ludus Capri out of the games and leave immediately.'

'I want to fight,' Almond said.

Everyone spun and stared at him.

'I want to fight in the arena and I want to fight against Ludus Leo.'

'I am sorry,' the lanista said. 'He is just a servant in my ludus.'

'Your servant and your gladiator, who is now dead, are the people who rescued the royal vampire and set the General's son free,' Almond yelled. 'I will not have you dismiss me.'

The General looked down at Hans's body and a second later it registered on his face. 'This is your gladiator. I remember him from the arena. A very gifted man.'

'It was Hans and I that went down to the Ludus Leo pet area and found the royal vampire,' Almond said. 'He defended me while I was setting her free. He must have stopped fighting when Erik appeared.'

'That is how he must have been bested,' the magistrus said. 'He would have put his guard down.'

The General looked at Almond. 'Your gladiator is dead. You cannot fight in the games.'

The lanista cleared his throat. 'I will take his place, sir. I will bring honour back to Ludus Capri.'

'Even if you had a gladiator, I am bringing the games to an end,' the General said. 'I have my son back.'

'Ludus Leo will say you have broken your word, General,' Almond said. 'They will want the keys to Battleacre.'

'Not to mention the citizens of Battleacre,' the General muttered. 'They will not accept an end to the games.'

'It is settled,' the lanista said. 'I will fight with my servant, Almond.'

The General turned to Almond. 'Again, I thank you for saving the royal. My son is on his way home. Is there anything the city of Battleacre can do for you?'

Almond thought for a second. 'I would like access to one of your smithies, General. An empty one.'

'It is done,' the General said. 'I will assign a workshop and inform your guard.'

Almond gave the General a nod. 'Thank you, General.'

The General turned and walked down the corridor.

The lanista let out a long sigh.

Almond turned and walked into the Ludus Capri cell. He dropped onto his blankets and curled up into a ball. Tears streamed down his face as he thought about his friend.

'Do you need anything, servant?' the magistrus said.

'I am fine,' Almond said, hiding his face.

The magistrus cleared his throat. 'I will wake you this evening.'

Almond listened to the magistrus's steps as he left the cell.

'It is time,' the magistrus said, nudging Almond with his foot.

Almond rubbed his eyes. He pulled on his sandals and stood.

'You look like you haven't slept at all.'

Almond glanced over to where Mahina and Jarod stood.

'I haven't,' Almond said, giving Mahina a small smile. 'Is it safe for you to be out here?'

'A lot has changed during the day,' Mahina said. 'Ludus Leo are keeping to themselves. The vampires have gone home and the General's son has returned.'

Almond smiled as Mahina turned a slight pink.

'Scrappy is waiting for us at the entrance,' Jarod said.

'How are you doing?' Almond said, casting an eye over the bruises on Jarod's face.

'I am doing fine,' Jarod said, lifting his chin. 'Mahina has been kind to me.'

Almond walked over to the cell gate. The guard unlocked it and let Almond pass. He beckoned for him to follow.

Almond, Mahina and Jarod followed the guard through the quiet corridors. They reached the ramp just as a barking Scrappy came bounding down. Almond knelt and caught the little dog in his arms. 'How are you, little one?'

Scrappy licked him all over his face.

'We need to get going, silly dog,' Almond chuckled.

The guard led them up the ramp and out into the night. To the north, the screams and shouts of laughter echoed down from the entertainment district. They turned south until they reached the road into the blacksmiths district. Turning right onto the main road, they followed the guard until he turned down a small alley.

'This is a bit scary,' Mahina said.

The guard looked over his shoulder. 'It is the only empty smithy.'

They reached an open door. The guard signalled for them to enter.

Almond walked in and looked around. 'This is perfect, thank you.'

The guard nodded and walked back to the door, where he stood with his back to them.

'What are you going to make?' Jarod said, as he walked around the workshop.

Almond walked up to a rack where thick leather aprons hung. He pulled one off, placed it over his neck, and tied the straps behind him. 'I am making weapons for myself.'

'Sit here and let Almond work,' Mahina said, signalling to the stool next to her.

Almond walked over to the furnace and lit it. He pumped air into the furnace until the fire burnt hot. Going through old weapons hanging on a rack, Almond selected several, which he then began to melt down. He searched the smithy for a short sword mould. He poured the molten metal into the moulds, then cooled it. He removed the blades and reheated them. The sound of metal striking metal echoed through the blacksmiths district.

Scrappy ran around the small smithy, sniffing out every corner. Jarod and Mahina sat chatting among themselves.

The hiss of metal hitting water sounded through the smithy. Almond removed the swords and began heating them again. The hours ticked by with the clanging sound of metal reverberating through the night. Almond turned and smiled at Mahina and Jarod, who were sleeping with their heads on the bench.

'Need to get them home, Scrappy,' Almond said.

The little dog wagged his tail.

Almond walked to the entrance and beckoned the guard. 'Can you escort these two to the carriage?'

'I have instructions to stay here,' the guard said.

'I will tell nobody,' Almond said, smiling. 'Just get back here before daybreak.'

The guard nodded.

'Come on, you two,' Almond said. 'It is time for you to go home.'

'I am awake,' Jarod said, his head popping off the bench.

Mahina yawned and stretched.

'Make sure your lady gets home safely, Jarod,' Almond said.

Jarod opened his eyes to protest, then looked at the half-asleep Mahina. With a sigh, he rose. 'Come on, my lady. We need to get back home.'

'You too, Scrappy,' Almond said, raising an eyebrow at the small dog.

Scrappy looked up at Almond and whined.

'I will see you soon, little one,' Almond said.

The guard disappeared up the alley with Mahina, Jarod and Scrappy.

Almond returned to continue making his swords. The moon slowly dragged across the sky. The guard eventually returned. Almond's muscles popped each time he slammed his hammer into the metal.

Just before dawn, Almond wrapped the two swords in cloth and walked up to the guard. 'Not anywhere near my best work, but not bad in the allotted time,' he said.

The guard took the two swords. He looked at Almond.

'What is it?' Almond said.

'I trust you will bring honour back to Ludus Capri,' the guard said. 'We have been the laughing stock for way too long.'

Almond rested a hand on the guard's shoulder. 'I will do my best.'

They left the smithy and went onto the main street. Blacksmiths turned their heads and bowed in greeting.

'We must hurry,' the guard said. 'We have to get there before the sun rises.'

They reached the gate of the amphitheatre just as the first sunray peeked over the horizon. Almond hurried down the corridors until he reached the Ludus Capri cell. He stopped and smiled at the lanista who stood in his gladiator outfit.

'I haven't worn this in years,' the lanista said. 'I just about fit.'

'You look like a true gladiator,' the magistrus said. 'Are you sure you do not want me to take your place?'

The lanista shook his head. 'I will die with honour and my debts paid, magistrus.'

'It is honourable, sir,' the magistrus said, slamming his fist against his chest.

The guard gave one gamekeeper Almond's swords.

Almond walked up to his blanket and sat.

The magistrus walked over with a tray of light food. 'Best eat light. A full stomach may hinder you.'

'How much time do I have?' Almond said.

'You are in the arena in three hours,' the magistrus said.

Almond finished the tray of food and lay on his blankets. No sooner had his head hit the small pillow, the magistrus was kicking him gently. 'It is time,' he said.

Almond walked up the ramp to the wooden doors. His lanista stood beside him. Despite his age, he looked fit and healthy.

'We will die with honour tonight,' the lanista said. 'I understand we have no chance against the two knife slingers.'

Almond looked straight ahead. 'I do not care about the knife slingers. Today, Ludus Leo pays for what they did to my friend.'

'And I shall assist,' the lanista said.

The wooden doors swung open. Trumpets sounded as Almond and the lanista walked into the arena. Across the way, Gron walked out with a grin on his face.

'He sees a telling victory,' the lanista said. 'Killing a lanista will be his greatest achievement.'

Almond continued walking to the centre. 'Where is the General's entry?'

The crowd quietened as a gamekeeper walked onto the podium. He read out the names of the ludi. A gasp sounded across the entire arena as the gamekeeper read out the gladiator of Ludus Capri as being the lanista. The crowd frantically got hold of their bookkeepers to change their bets.

The General walked onto the podium. He waited for the crowd to quieten. 'Citizens of Battleacre. I have removed my team from the tournament. Whoever should win today will receive a seat on the council as the Queen once ordered.'

Gron turned and sneered at the General. His lanista stepped forward, but stopped. He took a step backwards and muttered under his breath.

'We may yet have a chance,' the lanista said. 'It does not look like we have to fight the knife slingers.'

Almond ignored him. He turned his head sideways to look straight at Gron. With a chuckle, Gron dragged his finger across his throat.

The lanistae of the two houses left. Almond and his lanista jogged back into their quadrant.

'Gron is mine,' Almond said, pulling a short spear from the first panel. 'Watch my back.'

The lanista stared after Almond. 'It's supposed to be the other way around,' he yelled.

Almond dived into the battle, twirling his spear. Both gladiators, apparently sensing their demise, decided to work together. The lanista brought up Almond's rear, defending him from any surprise attacks.

'My fight is not with you,' Almond said, taking the other gladiator's legs. 'All I want is Ludus Leo.'

Gron swung his sword. Almond ducked. 'This gladiator is fighting to win, servant. He will not be listening to you.'

Almond felt a twinge of pain run across his left thigh. Looking down, he saw a trickle of blood. He dodged another sword attack and hopped back to where the lanista stood. His face red with effort, the lanista took another swing at a servant.

'Too quick for me,' the lanista said.

Almond took in a deep breath. 'I was hoping not to have to do this.'

The lanista squared up against the two servants.

Almond flicked the spear around and threw it with all his might. The other gladiator, expecting it to go for Gron, was slow to react. A second later, he lay on his back with the spear protruding from his chest.

'Run,' Gron shouted to the servant. 'Do not let them catch you.'

'He is keeping him in the fight so you cannot get your weapons,' the lanista said.

Almond squared up to Gron. He took the measure of the sword in his hands.

'You are a dead man,' Gron said, planting his feet into an attacking stance.

'Have you got his servant?' Almond said over his shoulder.

'Not for long,' the lanista said, blowing hard.

Almond ran at Gron, who swung his sword head-high in a wide arc. Almond ducked and skidded through the dirt. He ran to the dead gladiator and pulled out the spear. He took two more steps and flung it at the running servant. With a thump, the servant slammed into the wall with the spear protruding out of him.

Gron turned and ran for his quadrant.

Almond spun around just to see the servant drive his dagger into the lanista's thigh. The lanista hit the servant square on the jaw with an uppercut. Almond ran past and grabbed the lanista by the hand, dragging him to the quadrant. The lanista reached into the panel and pulled out a scimitar. Almond reached in and pulled out two shining short swords.

'I don't know how much longer I can last,' the lanista said.

'Just stay alive until I kill this gladiator,' Almond said.

The lanista struggled to his feet. 'Let us fight with honour.'

Almond walked slowly to the centre of the arena. Gron and his servant stood waiting. The servant whispered something to Gron, then peeled off to the side.

'He is coming for you,' Almond said.

The lanista stood up tall and readied his scimitar.

Almond ran towards Gron. 'Your time of dishonour has come, Gron. I will end you for my friend.'

'He was a weak man,' Gron said, swinging his hammer. 'I should have ended him long ago, but I took pity on him.'

'Your first mistake,' Almond said, darting in and slashing a gash along Gron's thigh, 'was to let him live.'

Gron winced and took a step back.

'Your second mistake,' Almond said, 'was thinking you could beat a knife slinger.'

Realisation streaked across Gron's face.

Almond stopped and pulled his legs together. He turned sidelong to Gron and extended his left arm. The knife-slinger stance.

Gron took a few steps back. 'This is not fair.'

Almond pointed his short sword at Gron. 'Hans dying in the corridors of this place was unfair. You dying in the arena is unfair. Nothing is fair in this world, Gron.'

A suck of air escaped the lanista's lips. Almond turned to see the servant pull out his weapon from the lanista's side. Almond darted in and dispatched the servant before he could react.

'I am OK,' the lanista said, rolling onto his back. 'Go and finish this.'

Almond stood and stared at Gron.

Gron looked at the wooden door that stood firmly shut.

Almond stalked Gron around the arena until they were near the podium. With a clash of steel, Almond and Gron fought.

'It doesn't matter,' Gron said, as he began to tire. 'My lanista will be head of Battleacre.'

Almond took a step back. 'What do you mean?'

Gron attacked with a flurry of hammer blows. Almond parried each, then struck with his short sword. Blood trickled down the blade as it entered Gron's side. Gron fell to a knee.

Almond walked up to him. 'What is your lanista planning?'

Gron smiled. 'It is too late.'

Almond took a step back and scanned the podium. He searched for Dimitri, who he signalled to. Dimitri stood and reached for his daggers. Suddenly, from out of the shadows near the podium, the Ludus Leo lanista rushed the General with several guards. Dimitri and Damsk went into action, protecting the General.

A thud sounded as the hammer slammed Almond square in the stomach. He flew through the air and slammed into the wall.

'Should have kept an eye on me, servant,' Gron said, hobbling towards Almond.

Almond tried to suck in air, but his body would not allow him to.

'I am not going to make this quick,' Gron said, twirling his hammer shaft in his hands.

'No, but I will,' the lanista said, driving his scimitar through Gron.

The light fled from Gron's eyes. The lanista fell face-first into the dirt. Darkness took Almond.

CHAPTER 8

A LONG TIME PASSED

Almond sat straight up. He winced at the pain in his stomach.

'The champion awakes,' the magistrus said.

'The lanista?' Almond said.

'He is doing just fine,' the magistrus said. 'He is with the medicus in the General's quarters.'

Almond lay back in his blankets.

'No rest for the wicked,' the magistrus said, walking over to Almond. 'The General has requested that you come and see him.'

Almond sat back up and dragged the blankets off his legs. He winced as he struggled to his feet. 'What happened after I passed out?'

The magistrus smiled. 'The crowd saw one of the greatest displays of knife slinger fighting known to Battleacre. Your brothers dispatched most of Ludus Leo.'

Almond dragged in a deep breath. He walked to the cell door, which lay open. The guard bowed his head.

'Good to see you again,' Almond said.

'Thank you for bringing honour back to Ludus Capri,' the guard said. 'Please follow me to the General's quarters.'

Almond followed the guard out of the amphitheatre and onto

the north–south road. The guard signalled and a minute later, a small horse and carriage pulled up. The guard opened the door, helped Almond in, and then sat next to him.

'I never caught your name,' Almond said, looking at the guard.

The guard smiled. 'My name is not important. We will be at the General's quarters shortly.'

Almond let his head rest against the carriage. He closed his eyes and remembered his friend, Hans. A few minutes later, the carriage stopped.

'We are here,' the guard said, stepping out.

Almond stepped out of the carriage and looked at the large house in front of him. 'The south-eastern district.'

'Yes, sir,' the guard said, opening the door and leading Almond up the steps. He knocked on the door.

'Good day, sir,' a man said. 'Can I help you?'

'Hello, Rafa,' the guard said. 'This is Almond, who is here to see the General.'

'I am pleased to meet you,' the young Rafa said. 'If you would follow me into the General's study.'

'I shall be waiting for you in the carriage,' the guard said, walking back down the stairs.

Almond followed Rafa into the study.

'I will bring you some tea,' Rafa said. 'The General will be with you shortly.'

Almond walked up to a side table and looked at the pictures. A young boy sat on the General's knee, smiling up at him.

'My son,' the General said, walking into the study. 'He wants to join the Queen's Guard and be a soldier one day.'

Almond smiled. 'What of Lady Mahina?'

The General smiled back. 'I am sure she will have a say in the matter. Please sit.'

Almond sat on one of the armchairs. The General walked up to a cupboard in the back of the study and pulled out items covered in cloth. He came and sat opposite Almond and laid the items on his knees.

'This is some of the best workmanship I have ever seen,' the General said, pulling out one of the short swords. 'And you did this in around eight hours?'

'From a time long passed, General,' Almond said. 'It is not what I do anymore.'

The General slid the sword back into the cloth and held it out for Almond.

'You can keep them both, General,' Almond said. 'All I wish to do is return home.'

'I am offering you your own smithy, Almond,' the General said. 'You may have the one you forged these in.'

Almond smiled. 'That is a kind offer, but I wish to get my dog and return to my house in the south.'

The General nodded. 'I understand.'

'Is everything OK in Battleacre?' Almond said.

'Everything is returning to normal,' the General said. 'It is the ludi that have caused issues. We are discussing abandoning them.'

'What of the gladiators and the Queen's Guard?' Almond said.

'It has long been said that we need to open the doors for all to fight in the arena,' the General said. 'We shall be closing down the ludi, but everyone will be allowed to fight in the arena.'

'After a few tests, of course?' Almond said.

'Yes,' the General said, smiling. 'It would be irresponsible to let just anyone fight.'

Almond nodded.

'I think that is us done, Almond,' the General said, extending his hand. 'If you change your mind, you know who to speak to.'

Almond extended his hand and shook the General's. 'Thank you, General.'

'Rafa, if you could escort Almond to his transport, please,' the General said.

'Yes, sir,' Rafa said, holding open the study door. 'Please follow me.'

Almond followed Rafa out of the General's house.

'It was a pleasure, Almond,' the General called.

Almond waved and walked up to the carriage. He opened the door, jumped in, and closed it behind him.

'Hello, Almond,' Genevie said.

Almond gasped in shock. 'Where is my guard?'

'Who, Gerald?' Genevie said, raising an eyebrow. 'He is out and about.'

'What do you want?' Almond said, a little too harshly.

'Strong words while speaking to a royal, Almond,' Genevie said.

He took in a breath. 'I am sorry, you just startled me.'

'Did you take the General's offer?' Genevie said.

'The smithy?' Almond said.

'Yes, the smithy,' Genevie said, smiling sweetly.

'No, I refused,' Almond said. 'I just want to return home with my Scrappy.'

Genevie folded her arms. 'I need you to reconsider.'

Almond looked at her in confusion. 'What is so important about me taking the smithy?'

'There is war, Almond,' Genevie said. 'War in the north from a dark force, even darker than our own. Mahina, Jarod, your lanista and Scrappy are all in danger.'

'Even more reason for me to go south then,' Almond said.

'We need you to create weapons when the time is right,' Genevie said. 'We need your skills, Almond.'

'I am sure there are enough blacksmiths here,' Almond said.

Genevie bared her teeth. 'I did not go through this whole fiasco to draw you out for nothing, Almond.'

Almond's eyebrows raised. 'You planned all of this?'

'Well, not all of it,' Genevie said. 'The getting captured part was not part of the plan. Getting you captured and taking you to Ludus Capri was.'

Almond's mouth hung open.

'That is all in the past,' Genevie said. 'I have news from your kin.'

'Do you mean my brother?' Almond said. 'Where is he?'

'City of Lynn,' Genevie said. 'He has something to give to you. He will be delivering it to you in the next few days.'

Almond sighed.

'Why don't you wait and see what he brings,' Genevie said. 'Then make a decision.'

Almond sighed again.

'Great, that's a deal,' Genevie said. 'Gerald, can you take Almond to the smithy?'

'Yes, my princess,' the guard said from outside the carriage door.

In a flash, Genevie was gone.

'Off to the smithy, then,' Gerald said.

Scrappy charged around the small smithy.

'Hello, Mr Almond,' Jarod said, running in.

'Please don't run around too much,' Almond said. 'There is dangerous stuff here.'

Jarod skidded to a halt. 'I found this for you.'

Almond took the flat cap from Jarod and placed it on his head. 'Thank you, Jarod.'

Scrappy barked at a small mouse, then chased it out of the smithy.

'How is everything with Mahina?' Almond said.

Jarod sighed. 'She spends most of her time at the General's house. It looks like she and his son are together.'

Almond chuckled. 'Jealous?'

Jarod shrugged. 'Well, at least I am no longer a slave. The ludus has all but been abandoned.'

'What will you do?' Almond said.

Jarod shrugged. 'I don't know. I might open a bar in the entertainment district.'

Almond chuckled again. 'I can certainly see you doing that.'

A knock sounded from the front of the smithy. A tall man stood with a hood covering his face.

'Go to the back, Jarod,' Almond said, while reaching for his short sword.

'What is it?' Jarod said.

'No more questions, boy,' Almond hissed. 'Get to the back.'

Jarod scampered into the back of the workshop.

Almond walked up to the man. 'Hello, brother.'

'Hello, Almond. I have brought you something courtesy of the vampires.'

Almond looked at the two small covered blocks on the cart. 'What are they?'

He lifted the cloth off the first block, revealing metal filled with a swirling cloud of white.

Almond gasped.

He lifted the cloth off the second block, revealing metal with a swirling cloud of black.

Almond's brother pulled the cloth over both blocks.

'I have fulfilled my debt.'

You have,' Genevie said from the shadows.

The man turned and stalked down the alley.

'I trust this means you will stay?' Genevie said.

Almond nodded.

Scrappy barked loudly.

NEXT UP...

Juno and the Lady (The Acre Series Book 1)

Juno's beloved Petra is dead.

Petra's replacement, the mysterious Lady, has put Juno's best friend Tilly under a dark spell that has left Juno with nobody she can trust.

With only Chax, her kitten, for company, Juno escapes from her school to a town at the bottom of the cliffs.

A town ruled by men.

Alone, scared, and without friends, Juno feels an unknown power growing inside her. A power she knows she will one day have to harness. With all lost, a dark figure from within the shadows cups her mouth and whispers in her ear to keep quiet.

Juno joins her new friends but just as she starts to learn how the world really works, the ill-tempered Dr Viktor demands an audience.

Juno and the Lady is a young woman's journey into a land of the old ways, where men rule, and women are property.

With unlikely friendships, forbidden love and burning magic, can Juno change the conventions of old? Can she save the town? And will she figure out who the Lady truly is?

AUTHOR REQUEST

Hello,
Thank you for taking the time to read **Almond and the Lanista**. It is the first prequel novella of Miles and the Soldier. I will be releasing more Miles novellas in the months to come.

If you have a moment, I would really appreciate a review on either Amazon or Goodreads. The reviews help us indie authors a great deal.

Please consider joining my mailing list where you will receive the FREE book, Dr Viktor and the Travelling Circus (BookHip.com/JDFLNKJ).

Again, thank you for spending your precious time reading my books.

Take care,
G.J.

ABOUT THE AUTHOR

A nomad at heart, GJ has lived in nine countries across Africa, Europe and the Middle East. His career has included working as a Divemaster in The Red Sea, a zookeeper in Israel, and a proofreader in Sweden. Born with cerebral palsy, GJ has spent a lifetime trying to tie his shoelaces while standing up in the hope of not falling over. It is a constant challenge, but sometimes he occasionally succeeds.

Finding the love for writing later in life, GJ spends most of his free time going for walks and dreaming of story ideas. He hopes to one day have a small place on the oceanfront where he can walk his dogs on the beach.

For more information please visit gjkemp.co.uk

facebook.com/gavin.kemp.92505
twitter.com/TB5Publishing
instagram.com/tb5publishing
linkedin.com/in/g-j-kemp-4a76b03
bookbub.com/profile/g-j-kemp

Printed in Great Britain
by Amazon